ARMS DEALS

For my partner in arms (control), Bill Hartung. Thanks for your advice on the plot, and for your work.

Caleb

ARMS DEALS

A MAR'SHAE MCGURK THRILLER
ABOUT
"SHOPPING TO GET YOURS"

BY CALEB STEWART ROSSITER

Design: Anne Masters Design

PRAISE FOR
ARMS DEALS

This rollicking and proudly politically incorrect thriller imagines an intersection between Washington DC's street gangs and the equally nefarious policy gangs that prosper on Capitol Hill. Along the way, Caleb Rossiter— a dedicated anti-imperialist and contratrian— humorously skewers just about everyone from the left-wing Weathermen to the neo-cons Elliott Abrams and Michael Ledeen.

—Kai Bird, *Pulitzer Prize-winning, humorless, and politically correct historian.*

For some years Caleb Rossiter was a key staff aide at the foreign policy caucus I chaired. We share a love of legal thrillers, and in this novel Caleb has drawn on his considerable knowledge of world affairs to tell a fascinating, page-turning tale.

—Matt McHugh, *congressman from New York, 1975-1993*

My former foreign policy staffer Caleb nailed it! He cleverly weaves a fast-paced tale of the two worlds I knew as a prosecutor and a member of Congress— criminals and DC lobbyists -- that share much in common. His dialogue is reminiscent of a George Higgins novel.

—Bill Delahunt, *congressman from Massachusetts, 1997-2011*

When my friend and long-time Capitol Hill colleague Caleb Rossiter published his first Mar'Shae McGurk thriller, *The Weathermen on Trial,* I felt obligated to get it and read it, even though I wasn't interested in the Weathermen and didn't expect great writing by a friend of mine. After a few chapters into that book, it became a page turner for me— right to the end. That would be reason enough to read the book, but another was his careful research and historical perspective. I learned much. I also recognized much about the federal bureaucracies, the politics of race, and the legal maneuverings with which I am familiar. And then too Rossiter's musicianship came through; he knows the music of the era. So now Professor Rossiter has published his second in what I expect will be a series of thrillers, and this time something that he and I worked for years to regulate and curb: the overseas transfer of lethal weapons for profit at the expense of human security. This new novel, *Arms Deals,* reveals of much that is hidden from the public and, at the same time, is an entertaining novel, "a good read."

—Joe Volk, *executive secretary emeritus, Friends Committee on National Legislation*

CONTENTS

CHARACTERS

REAL

Mahamadou Issoufou, *President of Niger, known as Zaki, "The Lion"*

Terry Crawford-Browne, *South African expert on corruption in the arms trade*

The Reverend Andrew Young, *civil rights leader, former ambassador*

The Reverend Jesse Jackson, *civil rights leader*

William Barr, *Attorney General*

Christopher Wray, *FBI Director*

Nancy Pelosi, *Speaker of the House*

Kevin McCarthy, *House Minority Leader*

Mitch McConnell, *Senate Majority Leader*

Chuck Schumer, *Senate Minority Leader*

FICTIONAL

General Walid N'Douro, *Defense Minister of Niger*

Mar'Shae "Black" McGurk, *FBI agent, daughter of Shaka-ette DuPlin*

Mary Olive DuPlin, *McGurk's grandmother*

Du'Shaunn Ruff, *McGurk's cousin, son of Mala'Tré Ruff and Ja'Liya Littlebrook*

Dr. Yates, *principal of DC's H. D. Woodson High School*

Major General Cal Jones, USAF (ret.), *consultant to Boeing*

Charlene Wong, *Mobe-Corp executive*

Kevin Smithson, *Aerospace Industries Association director of international sales*

Rachel Craig-Williams, *patrol officer, DC Metropolitan Police Department (MPD) Sixth District*

Samuel "USS" Solomon, *Craig-Williams' patrol partner*

La'Darius Ennis, *high school student, H. D. Woodson High School*

Tupelo Jones, *Clay Kings gang member*

La'Damien Cass, *homicide detective, MPD*

Shirley Tono, *Cass' partner*

Mary Magdalen Carter, *director, World Financial Transparency*

Pierre Nkumbo, *Africa Division Director, Human Rights Watch*

LaKisha Blunt, *professor, American University, Washington, DC*

Charles Hillard "Trey" Burr III, *director, FBI International Operations Division*

Jerome Cleaveland, *DC street criminal, incarcerated in Alexandria, Virginia*

La Shonda, *former Clay Kings accountant, federal prisoner, FCI Aliceville, Alabama*

Bobby LaGraux, *warden, FCI Aliceville, Alabama*

James Harris, *Clay Kings shot-caller*

Jan Bryant, *retired "Abscam" FBI agent*

Naomi, *policy activist, Institute for Policy Studies*

Jillian Krist, *Representative in Congress*

Bob DeWitt, *FBI task force leader*

Sharia Denby, *DC criminal lawyer*

Admiral F. D. Kirtland, *Chief of Naval Operations*

PART I:
THE TAKE

CHAPTER 1:
JANUARY 2019 – NIGER'S MAGIC DRAGONS

"Now the Americans want more. Not just to double the size of their Air Force base in Agadez, but to build another one for Langley, at that old commercial strip even deeper in the Sahara, in Dirkou. Really, how many drones does one country need? Allah protect us, the Americans never let up: I agreed to drone flights and a handful of Green Berets to pass the information to our Tuareg-hunters, and then next thing I know there's a thousand troops, and four of them dead!

"The other presidents say it's the same with them. The Americans only set up the African Command ten years ago, and made a big show about not being colonialists by basing its headquarters in Europe and not on the continent— and then quietly set up three dozen bases on the continent and they train and run exercises in all 55 countries.

"The press in America laughed out loud when that senator on the military committee said he had no idea there were U.S. troops fighting here. Well, I certainly didn't admit it, but I didn't know either! Mother of a goat— my son, would you please remind those camel-piss Indonesians not to bang those hammers when I'm in here?"

His Excellency Mahamadou Issoufou, the president of Niger, an impoverished landlocked country of 18 million with the lowest agricultural and highest female fertility in the world, switched from French and yelled the curse and request in Hausa to his secretary over the banging of hammers.

The Indonesian government was renovating the ancient French presidential palace in Niamey in return for Niger's vote for a two-year seat on the UN Security Council.

The secretary was sitting at his desk outside the presidential office where Issoufou, or Zaki, "the Lion," as he was referred to by all, was meeting with his long-time top general and hence coup protector, Walid N'Douro. The secretary wasn't actually the president's son. As in most African languages, reflecting joint responsibilities and loyalties throughout the tribe, family titles in Hausa also referred to all people of similar generations.

The reason the Lion had to raise his voice dramatically to make sure his secretary heard him was that the air conditioners were blasting in both of their offices. Niamey is tucked in the far south-western corner of the sprawling desert country north of Nigeria, in the relative coolness along the great Niger River, a thousand miles of jeep and camel track from the airstrip in Dirkou that the Americans now wanted for a base. Still, even relative coolness is relative.

It was the middle of winter, but at 10 a.m. it was already 32 degrees. High summer would bring that to a constant 38. The pecking order of power and coolness was being played out here as in all offices in Africa: the big man gets the best air conditioner and hence the most frigid room, and the temperature ascends as power descends.

Only a quarter of African homes have electricity, but presidents' offices never even have black-outs. Giant diesel engines out back simply snap on when, as on most days, the grid goes down for lack of power. The lung-shredding particulates they spew out are the legacy of the World Bank's ban on building modern fossil-fueled power plants, which "scrub" out nearly all pollution. The Western governments that control the Bank fear a long-predicted but never realized climate catastrophe from the heating effect of carbon dioxide, the powerful plant food that is a by-product of burning fossil fuels for energy. Instead they've created a present-day health catastrophe with this carbon colonialism, from the "dieselization" of Africa as well as from indoor air pollution due to cooking and heating with wood and dung.

Issoufou had been speaking French with N'Douro because their mother tongues, like the peoples who spoke them, could not have been more different. The Lion spoke the tonal Congo Basin language of the Hausa, a settled people that had long dominated Northern Nigeria and were now the majority in Niger. The general spoke Fulfulde, atonal and full of declensions, because he was of the Fulani, the legendary nomadic warriors and herders whose people sprawled thousands of miles east from its birthplace on the Atlantic Coast.

Britain's colonial administrators in the 19th century treated the two peoples as a single unit, calling them the Hausa-Fulani, since they were both Muslim tribes willing to accept indirect rule through their sultans. But that colonial fiction never caught on. Both men were proudly Nigerien, and also in many ways more French than the French colonialists who ruled directly in the 20th century and indirectly since then; but it would never have occurred to them that they were of the same people.

The president came from a noted Hausa clan. The effects of a childhood of French-style nutrition and medicine were evident in his tall, elegant carriage. The squat, gap-toothed general was up from rural poverty. He dubiously traced his male ancestors, whose busts sat on his mantle at home to inspire proper family behavior, back to Usman don Fodio, "the Teacher." Usman led the Fulani Jihad that conquered most of West Africa at the same time Napoleon Buonaparte was conquering most of Europe.

While French is still the official language in Niger (just as the Euro-linked "colonial" franc is still the official currency), it is a weak *patois* for the rural 80 percent of the country who live in traditional mud huts with little access to electricity and indoor plumbing. For the elite, though, it's second nature. Both men had taken their secondary schooling in French schools in the capital. Issoufou had then earned an engineering degree in Paris, and N'Douro had taken a physics degree in Niamey and numerous military courses in France. He'd also acquired a decent bit of English at Lackland Air Force base in Texas during the language courses for his many U.S. military training stints.

"Zaki, you'll remember well that we had little bargaining power with Obama on Agadez. The French were desperate for surveillance to help roll back the Islamists when they overran most of Mali. Of course, they had themselves to blame. The war only happened because Qaddafi's Tuareg mercenaries ran off with his weapons after BHL's 'light' NATO air war on

Libya— of course, I mean American air war, with NATO cheering— left a vacuum on the ground. But the French hand is one we never bite."

The president laughed: "Indeed, especially since they upped our uranium payments, after we caught them low-balling their profits. That's virtually our only source of hard currency now, until that British firm turns its lovely oil strike into a running well. But Allah knows, the Americans threatened to declare the desert an ungoverned space anyway, and just set up shop. And I wanted to track our own Tuareg bastards, so why not? It was a good deal for us in a lot of ways, even though we couldn't squeeze much foreign aid out of the Americans."

"Right," replied the general, "but now we can take care of that too. The war's essentially over in Mali. Once Qaeda took over with their crazy rules and made enemies even of the Tuareg, it was easy for the French to put them both back in the box. And Trump and Macron aren't like Obama and Sarko, the two musketeers, all for one and all that, sharing their favorite restaurants. Just to be sure, I called over to the "swimming pool" in Paris. The SE truly doesn't care, either way. This is really an ask, not a demand, from the Americans. Let's get what we want this time."

"My self-same thoughts, my brother," countered Issoufou, politely stressing his common age with N'Douro, although his presidential position would permit him to use "son." The hammering had mercifully shifted to a distant wing of the palace. "And just what do we want?"

"One thing and one thing only, father," said N'Douro, ritually declining the intimacy. "Puff the Magic Dragon. I want us to be the first to own and operate what the Americans have never given to anybody else."

"A Magic Dragon? Walid, what are you talking about? Is it a weapon? And why do we need it?"

N'Douro rose from his pillow and walked around as he talked. "It's an American warplane, the AC-130. The Air Force calls it the Spectre or the Spooky, and pilots call it the Angel of Death. But the grateful soldiers on the ground watching it do its work have always called it Puff. It's like that one huge American cargo plane we have, the C-130, but in the Armed-Cargo configuration, built heavy to handle the weapons. It mounts two of the most powerful rotating machine guns in history, sticking out of one side, each firing up to 6,000 rounds a minute, and an awesome anti-vehicle cannon, 200 rounds a minute. Praise Allah, the Americans even put a field howitzer on it, but we'd have no use for something that big.

"Puff circles slowly in a pylon turn, a long arc high over the battlefield, with propellers because jets are too fast. It flies much higher and so is much safer from ground attack than helicopters, like the Soviets used in Afghanistan before the rebels got hand-held ground-to-air missiles. Its computer factors in speed, course, and altitude and directs the two guns as they swivel and place bullets, believe this or not, on every square meter of a FIFA pitch in about half a minute. The computer can set that to a tighter or looser fit, of course, and the Magic Dragon can hover over a battle, firing when needed, for hours.

"It's a beautiful thing, absolute dominance when the enemy doesn't have aircraft. Without it, the Americans might never have pacified Iraq, or held on in Afghanistan. They would've had to use bombs and artillery to go after the enemy, with far more collateral damage and civilian death, and that's what really turns people against you.

"We always joke about Puff as our Holy Grail of arms sales at our command staff meetings with AFRICOM. Reagan let the Salvadoran Air Force use the smaller, older version of the Magic Dragon, the AC-47, against guerrillas in their civil war. American gunners went on most of those missions because the Pentagon lawyers worried that the Salvadoran Air Force would massacres civilians, just like their Army did from the first day of the civil war to the last. And nobody, not even NATO, has gotten the Spooky, the AC-130.

"But Trump is a whole new half of football. All the presidents after Reagan have beaten their predecessors' records on world arms sales, but he's pushed the Pentagon to sell virtually anything made in the USA. We would have to agree in writing to use Puff only in desert battles, but you know from the Saudis in Yemen and the Israelis in the West Bank just how strictly the Americans enforce those types of agreements. Look, Zaki, somebody's going to be first, and I want it to be us."

"Very well," the president replied. "I like the idea, I can see how it would freeze our restless northern trouble-makers in place, and I can already hear the baying of the local business partners the Americans would need for the wonderful training and maintenance contracts such a weapon would require, let alone the offsets. But slow down, I'm a bit lost. Why is it called Puff, and why also a Magic Dragon?"

"Right, right," went on N'Douro. "Well, there was apparently an American radio song in the 1960s about a magic dragon named 'Puff,' and the troops in Vietnam first used that name for a makeshift version of the AC-47, because of the fire and smoke that surround the guns when they're firing. On the much bigger AC-130, which came on line later in the war, it's even more spectacular. Let's watch it on YouTube and you'll see what I mean."

Issoufou yelled again for the secretary, who called up a video on his computer. The two men watched in awe as a Spectre circled at 7,000 feet and in just a few seconds eviscerated ground structures with the miniguns and then old vehicles with the cannon. After thinking for just another few seconds, the president approved the plan: "Well of course, you're right. And I bet we can do better on offsets and local support contracts than we did with the French the last time around. It's a Lockheed-Martin plane, like our C-130, right? I met the CEO when we bought that one. He should be happy to push Trump to sell us some more."

"Well, he's not really going to be the player in this," said N'Douro, "The heavy lifting would be done by our friends at Boeing, who sold us our $40 million presidential jet. They take the heavy-frame Spectre from Lockheed and add the business end, the guns and cannon, and especially the computers and mounts needed to run them.

"You see, the aircraft itself is actually the least of the cost. We can get a new AC-130 for around $20 million, maybe up to $30 million depending on the flight and radar packages, and there are good used ones out there too. But the lethal fixings cost probably another $160 million per plane. And the training and maintenance contracts on a few Puffs? Probably more still."

"Well of course, we're getting new Magic Dragons," laughed Issoufou, "because if the Americans want the drone bases as much I think they do, we won't be paying for them! I forget the exact amount of U.S. aid we're getting now, but it's not much, maybe 100 million CFA a year, and most of it for food relief for the Tuaregs in the drought region, which doesn't do much for me down here in Niamey. So tell them they can make it free, or as one of those long-term military loans that somehow get forgiven in the out-years.

"We had to make the progress payments in cash for the 737, although the Americans did give us their Export-Import Bank break on interest. But we're not paying anything for these. And make sure we're set up for the service contracts to be covered too, for years. Get a proposal to AFRICOM, but make no mention of any link to the CIA's request. That would be rude, and even insulting. They'll know it's a package without us rubbing their noses in it.

"And I don't care if we're not paying for it. From the companies' perspective, it's still an arms sale and we expect the same offset sweeteners and local contracts from them that come with cash sales. I know we haven't bought many weapons there, but I'm sure you know somebody from all your time at those Pentagon schools who can give us some good advice, for a price.

"But let's push it through Washington as soon as possible. Right now, because I went to the Charlie Hebdo march and let the Italian Army in to block the migrant road to the coast, I'm the West's best friend, the new Kagame. But remember, Kagame himself was the new Museveni, until the new wore off of his crystal chandelier, too. And I'm stepping down after my second term in 2021 without messing with the constitution like Tanja did—a $5 million Ibrahim prize for leaving office after my term beats a coup every time! So as our French friends say, we need to dig for truffles while the pigs are hungry. Now if you'll excuse me, Walid, I'm leaving for the weekend palace, so these Indonesian imbeciles can finish up all the sooner."

CHAPTER 2:
FEBRUARY 2019 – BLACK HISTORY MONTH

Special Agent Mar'Shae "Black" McGurk turned the semi-armored black Chevy Suburban into the parking lot at Howard Dilworth Woodson High School, way "east of the river" at the tip of the diamond-shaped District of Columbia. She'd left her own car back in her space under the FBI building on Pennsylvania Avenue in Northwest, figuring that a cherry 2012 *Laguna Seca* Boss Mustang 302 wouldn't last long unattended in Northeast, particularly at HD. Black with red trim, she thought, built to be barely street-legal, and flaunting an X-brace stabilizer where the rear seat should be? Please, child.

On a tip from a friend at DEA, Black had snatched up the Boss at a drug-seizure auction for $10,000. She figured it could easily be worth a Big Benjamin to the car rings that shipped exotic rides to Latin America on the same day they were grabbed. When she was at the old HD, before a no-maintenance budget finally brought the seven-story Tower of Power's vaunted escalators to a halt, she would've known exactly whom to call if she'd seen something like that in the lot.

Black got out of the Suburban. She looked good, she thought, for a 30-something from Northeast: tall, jacked up, with stylish short hair midway between process and 'fro, shoes that were slick on top and gripped on the bottom, her trademark black pantsuit that made people wonder if she were gay and her trademark stone face to strangers that made them afraid to ask, great leather duster…she was clearly employed at something better than doing nails. And Black felt good, too. She'd just made major bones in her first assignment in the Emmett Till "Cold Case" unit. That had earned her a ticket into Public Corruption, of Abscam fame, where reputations were made forever by taking down politicians, the bigger the better.

This was actually the first time Black had seen the new HD, a gleaming $100 million gem. The parking lot overlooked the sort of pricey athletic facilities she'd expect at private schools "west of the park" in wealthy, white far Northwest: a pretentiously-named "Natatorium," ten tennis courts, and a turf-field football stadium. Black had left for the Army in 2006, two years before the Tower's demolition, and had done her best to avoid coming east of the river since she got out in 2012.

It wasn't that she was worried about running into the girls she'd cut drugs with back in the day. There'd been no hiding her ghetto past from the FBI, and three successful years on the job had turned it into a helpful curiosity on her career path rather than a liability. It was just that there was literally nothing there for her— no restaurants, no movie theaters, no clubs, no appreciating property values, no nothing for the 300,000 low-income black residents stuck between the Anacostia River and the wealthier black enclave of Prince George's County, Maryland.

And coming over to Northwest for dinner sure didn't seem to bother her granny Mary Olive DuPlin, who had raised her, or the five teenage grandchildren she was still raising in her 60s. While they rarely left the comfort of their Simple City neighborhood on Benning Heights on their own, they were eager to pass up the usual bullet-proof glass counters at Chinese take-outs and the Shrimp Boat, and cross the river on the metro to hit the Chipotles, Fuddruckers, and Johnny Rockets with Auntie Mar'Shae.

They could count on Black to know how to navigate the booming areas like Gallery Place, Columbia Heights, and U Street, which had only recently been revitalized from the King riots by metro stops and white millennials who bought the new condo apartments with parental money. The kids especially liked roaming the aisles of the fancy food store, Whole Foods, across from her apartment building on P Street. Their game was to pick up something, like a tiny $10 bottle of fresh kale juice, and announce its equivalent at the Safeway on Minnesota Avenue:

"Three six-packs of 16-ounce Pepsi, on sale for $7.50."

Black flashed her FBI creds and walked past the metal detectors, smiling as she remembered how her set had managed to sneak drugs, knives, lighters, beepers, and even massive, first-generation mobile phones past the screeners and into the Tower. Security looked a little better now, with a dozen smartly-dressed guards at the entrance, backed by two police officers and a couple of guys from the Goon Squad. That's what staff and students alike called the mid-twenties former HD football players who were hired to enforce order, since private security wasn't allowed to move students by force or even hit them back. Still, Black thought it was unlikely that she and the officers were the only people in the building carrying a weapon.

"Good afternoon. Mar'Shae McGurk, to see Principal Yates," Black said to the ancient secretary. "Hmmm. Yes, I thought I knew that name when I saw it on the announcement for the assembly," she replied. "I remember you, child, and that rascal mother of yours, barred from the school for cursing the guards! Lord have mercy, no team player, that one." She walked off to look for the principal. Lord have mercy is right, thought Black; no wonder I never come back. Her cousin Du'Shaunn Ruff saved her from the sort of sharp response she would have snapped out back in the day. He burst through the office door and yelled, "Auntie Mar'Shae! Black is back, niggah, and you the star today!"

Indeed she was. That was the whole point: HD alum makes good as FBI agent, comes to school in black pantsuit showing the holstered Glock 17M and extra mag (just in case the first 17 bullets don't do the job, as Jerry Cummings, her first supervisor, loved to say), inspires students to greatness. How did she ever get involved in this? Ah, right, Du'Shaunn won a pizza by entering her name in a "successful graduates" contest for the Black History Month assembly the school put on each February. Technically, that was a bit off, since after her senior year Black had blown off the usual summer school "credit recovery" courses, refusing to show up even the few times that were needed for a D. She'd gotten her GED in the Army. Later came a B.S. at George Mason on the Army's dime, and now she was back at Mason in the evenings, getting the master's in public policy she needed to stay on track at the FBI.

As they hugged Black joned him a bit: "Boy, what's up with this school?

It's all Rock Creek Park! A Nat-a-tor-i-um? Tennis? Who the hell is that for? And a "stadium" 'stead of a football field? Byron Leftwich and Kenny Crawley still be runnin' 'round these nasty streets?"

"Oh, no worries, we still ghetto. The pool be closed, 'cause they can't afford the cleanin', and nobody uses them tennis courts 'cept the dog-fighters, even after Serena Williams came by with the Mayor's wife."

Du'Shaunn, whose name was one of a dozen variants on DeSean in the school that were all pronounced the same, was a handsome, lanky, and carefully-groomed 14-year-old. His short hair was carefully razor-parted, with patterns of the Sun and planets etched on the sides. His starched and ironed white t-shirt was literally radiant with bleaching, and the blue jeans that hung well down off his waist were creased like a knife's edge. While Du'Shaunn's Nike basketball shoes were one model behind the curve, at his grandmother's insistence for his safety, he painstakingly cleaned them every night and often had them professionally prepped with the "hustle money" his father, Black's uncle Mala'Tré Ruff, randomly brought by for him.

"But the 'ball-field," he continued, "that's indeed the place. Kids can't find a seat 'cause my pops and all the other OGs pack it Friday nights and tell lies how they almost made it out."

Black silently reflected on the irony of the absent fathers, the "Original Gangsters," somehow finding time to get to school for the games. None of her friends coming up had a dad or even a step-dad in the house, and her own father was a mystery. Her mother Shaka-ette, just 14 when Mar'Shae was born, claimed that all she knew about the sugar daddy one of her friends introduced her to for an afternoon's sex was that his last name was McGurk. Mary Olive had pulled her own act together by then, at 31. She simply took over the role of mother to Mar'Shae, along with the AFDC support payments for both her daughter and granddaughter. She'd been doing that for Du'Shaunn too, since his mother, Mala'Tré's squeeze Ja'liya Littlebrook, died of AIDS when he was five.

Unfortunately, Shaka-ette never did pull her act together. At 20 she went to prison for possession of crack cocaine with intent to distribute. The prosecutors had overcharged her to force her to snitch on the dealer she was carrying one rock for on a Greyhound bus from DC to Raleigh, but she'd imbibed the neighborhood mantra: "Snitches gets stitches and winds up in ditches."

Shaka-ette's defense attorney's closing argument was essentially that Black's mother's testimony showed that she wasn't smart enough to intend to do anything. The judge formally instructed the jury to disregard that possibility in their deliberations, since only evidence of poor grades and dropping out rather than actual retardation had been introduced. DC juries had a history of "nullifying" in those days. One had famously ignored an instruction from a judge to find the Mayor (which east of the river always means the now-late Marion Barry, not the current official) guilty of smoking crack cocaine, as shown on an FBI video. "The bitch set me up" by refusing to have sex until he had used the crack, the Mayor told the FBI during the arrest. The judge ruled that this didn't constitute illegal "entrapment," but the jury wasn't buying it. It acquitted the Mayor on that charge, although it brought him down for another incident, and he served six months

Shaka-ette wasn't so lucky. She became a Lorton woman, serving five years in DC's suburban Virginia prison right before it closed in the late 1990s. Since Lorton she'd cycled between using, tricking, jail, hospitals, clinics, and half-way houses. Mary Olive threw her daughter out after a couple of years of that. As she sternly told a bewildered 13-year-old Black at the time, it takes a former drug whore to know when a current one can't get out. That was the closest Mary Olive ever got to acknowledging the neighborhood tales about Wilbur London, a DC cop convicted in the early'70s for running a stable of underage prostitutes.

"Ah, Mala'Tré! How is that old rascal?" Black cringed as she realized she'd jokingly used the same nasty street term for Du'Shaunn's father that the secretary had with all seriousness used for her mother. "I mean, you know, does he keep up with the other two? That go-go band?"

Malachi Ruff, a muffler installer at Goodyear who was the rare working man in Simple City, had been Mary Olive's man after her "lost years," as she called her drug-driven teens. He already had two boys, Mala'Uno and Mala'Two, living with two different mothers, so of course he named his son with her as number three. The informal deal in Simple City was then, and is now, that a man who stands by a teenage girl through birth gets to name the boys, but not the girls, which is seen as the special provenance of young mothers. Malachi wasn't with Mary Olive too long after that, but they remained friends, sometimes going to see the Chuck Brown-style rhythmic dance band the three half-brothers had formed when they were at HD.

"Oh Tré, he good. Still talkin' 'bout Saint Aug's, could'a done this, could'a done that hadn't hurt his knee, but he on a truck now, drivin' for Sanitation. The OGs don't play out too much, but some." Unlike his half-sister Shaka-ette and his two Mala half-brothers, Mala'Tré had done the minimal work needed to graduate from HD. He went on to Saint Augustine's, an historically-black college in Raleigh, on a football scholarship, but was quickly overwhelmed by the non-credit remedial courses he had to take in English and math. By December he was home with a tall tale about how the coach had taken away his scholarship because he'd missed practices with a sprained knee.

"Agent McGurk, I'm Dr. Yates. Thanks for coming. The mayor makes us have monthly assemblies, like she said she had at Elizabeth Seton, the private school she went to, but it's nice when we can actually have someone the kids can look up to and learn from." Yates was a chunky, mid-40s man with a gleaming bald head, wearing shirtsleeves and a fat tie in the African colors of green, red, and black. Black thought he seemed more relaxed than the principals she remembered, especially when he cracked, "I always think about taking a sick day when assembly rolls around, but your talk is one I really want to hear!"

Yates led her and Du'Shaunn past a wild scene at the doors of the auditorium. Anticipating the 2 p.m. assembly that was also going to feature a student fashion group called the Ladies of Distinction, students had been slipping out of classes to get front-row seats, from which they could best shriek their appreciation. All the Goon Squad was at the one open door, arms locked and screaming that nobody would be admitted without their teacher, and to go back to class. Yates slid through to an unmarked side door, which he opened with a key from the massive collection hanging on a lanyard around his neck. He explained to Black that he also had an electronic key, coded to allow him all-access, but that it worked so rarely than he just went old-school automatically.

The teachers had been instructed to walk their students down in a quiet single file when called over the intercom, just like in the fancy schools and indeed just as they had done in their neighborhood elementary school. But those days were gone. Some of the intercoms were out, the secretary forgot to call some classrooms, and as teachers saw fewer and fewer students in their room, they just released them all. Soon the mob at the one door precluded any effort to let in even the few teachers who had kept a group of students near them on the walk down, so the GS popped all the doors and let the students run in.

Black and her cousin sat on the stage as Yates tried to bring the house to order. As was typical, about half the seats were filled, since about half of HD's students skipped school each day. The teachers ignored a plea for them to sit with their classes, since their students were dispersed, and just sat in the back of the hall. The Goon Squad roamed the aisles, muscling into the rows to remove yelling or shoving students who were pointed out to them by an assistant principal walking back and forth on the stage. There was no discussion and no hesitation. If someone was pointed out, they knew that the GS wouldn't back down. Most came voluntarily, and a few were dragged out, all to the hoots of their peers, who were largely engrossed in their phones.

The special education teacher who coached the Ladies of Distinction strode to the center of the stage carrying a microphone. She was an ample woman with a full-length dress and a short blonde haircut who exuded confidence in every stride and every glance. The students screamed and whooped for her as she did a little dance. "Warr-eee-ooors, Warr-eee-oors," she and the students chanted over and over, louder each time, in a call and response. Images of the school's mascot flashed on and off on the jumbotron screen behind her. This is one place, thought Black, where the controversy over Native American team names like the Redskins will never be an issue! The muscle-bound Warrior was a Zulu, stabbing with his assegai from behind a cow-hide shield in the same African colors as the principal's tie.

The lights on the stage dimmed to a soft purple and the female students erupted into a desperate keening and the male students into a barking chorus as a long line of young women strutted slowly onto the stage.

The Ladies carefully placed each foot down to jerk their hips to one side and then paused a counted second before placing the next foot down and sashaying to the other extreme. They were shoed in the highest of heels, to accentuate their motion, and dressed in elegant but provocative sheer gowns, revealing all of their figures, ranging from anemic to corpulent. For 15 minutes they moved slowly around the stage in intricate patterns to a thumping beat, somehow both innocent and sexual at the same time, before leaving to a renewed call and response of "War-eee-ors."

As the shouting subsided to a buzz, Yates walked to the podium. "This here is one of us, y'all," he said, ignoring the prepared biography that the FBI public affairs team had written for him. "Give it up for Mar'Shae McGurk, FBI agent." Black stood at the podium, and pointed to the technician in the back, who started up the slides she'd recently presented in class at George Mason as course work. Quite a contrast in audiences for the same talk, she thought.

"Good morning, Warriors! My unit enforces the Hobbs Act, which means we chase corrupt officials, like mayors and senators, who steal when they're supposed to be serving you. I just started there a few months ago, after three years in the Emmett Till "Cold Case" unit for murders during the Civil Rights marches down South in the 1960s." This opening had no effect on the hum of talk or the faces looking at phones. Flummoxed, Black tried the joke that had worked so well for her professor on the first day of PowerPoint.

"Hey, how many of you know how to make a PowerPoint presentation?" A few hands went up. "Do you know what somebody who doesn't know PowerPoint says to someone who does?" A bit less humming. "Do you want fries with that?" A few oohs and snickers, but the humming went back on full mode. So Black used her HD history teacher's old trick of looking directly at the one student who seemed to be listening, and ploughed through the slides in ten minutes, ending with "Does anybody have any questions?"

For the first time, the auditorium approached silence, as the students looked around to see who might speak up. They were rewarded when a tall and broad boy stood up in the center of a group of athletes wearing garish HD leather football jackets. "Congo, Congo," the students began to chant. The boy smiled and waved, and as the laughter died down turned back to Black.

"You ever smoke anybody with that Gat?" The public affairs people had warned Black that this was probably a question she'd hear in some form from any group of kids, so she was prepared.

"Well, that's a fair question. First, this is not a Gatling gun. That means a machine gun that fires continuously, hundreds of bullets a minute. I used those when I was in the Army, in Afghanistan, because we're at war with people who are trying to destroy America and our freedom. ('What freedom?", sang out a laughing voice, to much applause.) My sidearm is a gun that fires a single shot at a time, as fast as I can pull the trigger each time, until the magazine runs out at 17 shots. The difference is important. We're not at war here, we're protecting the public. We use our weapons to make arrests of people who are a danger to you, that's it. And no, I've never had to fire my weapon as an FBI agent."

Congo was still standing. "But then in the army? You ever wasted anyone?" There was some tittering and cheering for Congo's boldness, but that died away quickly.

Black reached for the misdirection that Public Affairs had suggested. "In war you shoot at the enemy, sure. But it can happen at long range, with a lot of noise and chaos. So usually you're never really sure what you hit. It's not like in the movies." She was not about to talk about the horror of the bodies left by firefights to defend her trucks after landmine explosions, where there was no "usually" about it: death was up close and personal on both sides, disfigured by the most ingenious technologies human beings could devise from the advances of science.

As Congo sat down, she noticed a stirring in some of the middle rows, and a low murmur. Uncertain about its cause, she paused. Yates leapt up and signaled to the GS, pointing to the doors in the back. Not again, he thought, not again. In boring assemblies he expected it, but not when you have the ladies strutting and an FBI agent showing off her gun. But the murmur started again, and got louder and more distinct: "Outside, outside, outside…" Suddenly, as the Goon Squad and the security guards lined up, locking arms across each of the doors, nearly all of the hundreds of students rose from their seats and started running toward the doors. The GS fought gamely but, like the British at Isandlwana in 1879 who were overwhelmed by the superior numbers of that Zulu Impi, they eventually crumbled.

Within minutes the students streamed through the auditorium doors, down to the front doors, and out onto the street. Students were not allowed to bring coats and bags into an assembly, so if there was any expectation of homework being done for the next day, teachers would have to waive it. Afterwards, Black asked Yates, "What was that about? I mean, HD was a rowdy place when I was here, but I've never seen that before!"

"Are you kidding? This is just my second year here, and that's about the tenth time I've lost control to the bum rush. That's why I hate the assemblies, and always put them in the afternoon so we don't lose a whole day if the rush comes. And don't get me started on the homecoming parade through the neighborhood! That one's like a rolling crime wave. 6-D has to drive ahead, trying to guess which snack shop the kids are gonna flash-mob."

CHAPTER 3:
MARCH 2019 – MAKING THE DEAL

General Walid N'Douro strolled past the Piazza Colonna on a frosty and bright Rome morning. For some reason he'd never understood, a statue of Saint Paul, added 1,400 years after the fact, looked down from the top of the column celebrating the now-displaced emperor Marcus Aurelius' victory over the Germanic tribes. The first thing the general noticed as he turned into the bright, spare Illy coffee shop just off the piazza was the security. Three large men stood at different corners of the front room, scanning and rescanning the clientele.

Even before N'Douro saw the tiny comm devices in their ears and clipped to their collars he knew them by the tight leather jackets that were difficult to grab and hold. These were the front men, without weapons, whose job it was to use muscle to resolve minor threats, like nosy reporters and picture-takers, and calmly submit to arrest if things got ugly. That meant there'd also be an armed team outside, probably in an unmemorable, much-used service van, in case of real emergencies, like a kidnapping. And of course there was a table of geeks by the gelato counter, sipping espresso and chatting brightly to distract people from the large satchels at their feet that contained powerful electronic jammers. Well, he thought, Mobe-Corp can afford it. As the largest private military contractor in the world, feeding off the out-sourcing of the biggest military spender in the world, they've got the money and the mercenaries to burn.

The rest of the tables in the front room were occupied by business-women on one of the semi-official Italian morning cappuccino breaks. Ah, Rome, thought N'Douro, where women still dress to kill. London and Paris may have collapsed under modern sloth, but sweatpants and sweaters will never come to Rome and Vienna! Looking around from the front room he saw Cal Jones waiting in the back room, at the cheap Formica tables by the espresso bar, with an elegantly dressed woman he assumed was Charlene Wong. Spiked heels, spiked hair, aerobic body, tailored suit with a skirt short enough to stop traffic even in Rome, if not Caracas. Praise the Prophet, he thought, life is good.

N'Douro's first call after the meeting with Zaki had been to General Jones, the Air Force officer who'd befriended him at the Lackland, Texas, language school during his first U.S. training tour 30 years ago. Cal was brushing up on his college-level French for an assignment as attaché in Paris and Walid was brushing up on his high-school English for flight training. Cal readily admitted he had been assigned to connect with the Nigerien, since the International Military Education and Training program had found that honesty was the best policy for a long-term relationship.

For the Pentagon, the military training that officially justified the program for congressional funding was incidental to the real purpose of IMET. It was primarily an intelligence program that made connections that would provide access to the foreign officers in later years. The Defense Intelligence Agency maintained a database of tens of thousands of them who'd been through IMET, tracking their assignments over the years along with those of their U.S. military pals. When a military or covert operation required cooperation with another country, this provided an immediate, personal point of entry. Even retired U.S. officers were eager to reconnect for a bit of air travel and per diem.

Walid hadn't cared about his new friend's motivations anyway. He was a professional too, with his own instructions to make connections for future initiatives. IMET trainees were allowed to save their stipend and buy and import one vehicle from the United States, and he and Cal had bonded over the lengthy deliberations about make and model. They settled on a softly-used, 1985 heavy-frame Ford F-series pickup with a tape deck, air conditioning, and a front stabilizer bar that held up for 15 years on the Nigerien dirt roads.

Cal and Walid had stayed in touch as they both climbed the ranks to become generals. Cal had retired as a two-star five years before. He immediately went to work as a defense consultant, moving between companies as the situation required, based on the contacts he had made in his career, both overseas and in Pentagon acquisition posts. When Walid explained the Spooky plan to him, he reconnected with Boeing and, for expenses and a contingency fee that escalated based on final value, came on board to make the deal. Cal knew Boeing would need a contractor to implement the deal's huge continuing component for training and servicing. He decided to bring in Mobe-Corp through Charlene Wong, who'd been his comptroller in one of his Pentagon acquisition posts.

Cal and Charlene were well aware that both parts of the deal would bring on a feeding frenzy of corruption, but they also knew how to insulate themselves and their companies from it. First, there would be the payments to private Nigerien facilitators. These were legal under the Foreign Corrupt Practices Act, but would inevitably lead to some of the cash being passed on covertly to government officials sitting at real and fictional regulatory bottlenecks. The amounts involved, though, paled in comparison to the massive, direct bribes by arms exporters to kings, princes, and prime ministers during the good old pre-FCPA days. The difference had quickly been made up by a convoluted set of arrangements called "offsets."

These are agreements by the arms-exporters to buy commercial goods and services from the purchasing country to help it "offset" the cost of buying and maintaining the weapons. There was much irony in Niger demanding an offset for this sale, since the purchase cost would be covered by a long-term U.S. Foreign Military Financing loan. All parties knew that the loan would be quietly forgiven a few years down the line as a late-night addition to a must-have Continuing Resolution appropriation that Members of Congress have neither the interest nor the ability to slow down.

Boeing would offer the offsets for purchases of aircraft, avionics, and weaponry, and Mobe-Corp would offer them for the training and service contracts. And then the great game would begin, as officials at the government's offset companies not only got away with charging high prices, but then over-priced and under-priced various trade invoices to separate cash from their own companies. And the cash would flow to the top, just like in the bad old days.

For example, a newly-formed Nigerien tourism parastatal might sell $10 million of global advertising services to a Boeing-funded offset business, a hotel venture in Niamey, and submit two invoices of $5 million each. Only one payment would be reported to the Nigerien Central Bank and converted to CFA francs for the local salaries of the staff designing commercials for the internet. Boeing would be told to deposit the other $5 million, supposedly for American consultants on media strategy, into the bank account of a Delaware shell company. The identities of the true "beneficial owners" are by law shielded, even from federal regulators. Only the local lawyer's name is registered. And of course, lawyers must respect their clients' wishes on confidentiality.

There would, of course, be very little in the way of a media strategy. Most of the money would be wired to an off-shore account and disappear forever from the control of both countries' regulators. A flurry of purposeful errors and replacement invoices, mimicking the daily corrections in legitimate international transactions, would further mask the rake-off. In the end, Boeing might even build the hotel for $25 million, while claiming a total investment of a few hundred million dollars to meet its offset agreement. It might even make some money, paying itself for its own contractors and staff visits, or selling the hotel to an international chain for a profit. Nobody in Niger would complain, because the government would frown on inquiries into any aspect of the deal.

This sort of gaming of taxes, tariffs, and invoices, known as "transfer pricing," moves trillions of dollars into and out of the black market every year, making a mockery of countries' attempts to collect taxes and control capital flight, let alone stop money laundering by drug smugglers and other illegal businesses. By the design of their own cash-hungry governments, the regulators are always kept a step behind the transfer pricers.

Individual Boeing and Mobe-Corp officials might be paid a bit to look the other way, but most of the siphoned money would end up in the offshore accounts controlled by Nigerien officials who ran or sanctioned the offset firms. The American companies themselves didn't need the scams, since the profit margins on military contracts are already significant. They would have clean books, unmarked by the side-deals. Treasury Department investigators run computer checks for strange invoice patterns and generate millions of Suspicious Activities Reports each year, overwhelming their investigative resources. They'd be unlikely even to open a file on an offset of this size. The legendary illegal arms broker, Victor Boot, who operated on a far greater scale, was only caught because someone, perhaps a competitor, had stolen and leaked his shell company's records.

Pointing to the phalanx of physical and electronic security personnel, N'Douro adopted the Godfather's gravelly voice and said, "Cal, my brother, what have I ever done to make you treat me so disrespectfully?" Jones laughed and replied, "I'm sure it's not you Charlene is worried about. Charlene Wong, meet Walid N'Douro. Please put him at ease." He couldn't resist his own Godfather imitation, from another scene with the disrespectful undertaker: "I want you to use all your powers and all your skills to protect Walid."

An assistant of Charlene's went to the counter to get an espresso for Walid, and the three of them sat down. "Are you kidding? Look, for deals like this, it's like Nixon said during Watergate: 'You could get the money fairly easily.' There's no reason we can't swing this one, and we all go home happy and rich. But Nixon was saying that on tape, and look what happened!

"So, yes, we do all we can to keep our cards close until it's time to lay them down. We're in Italy, after all, the wild west, land of Machiavelli and Michael Ledeen. Nobody really controls SISMI and its many power channels, and I'm sure the swimming pool's been watching you since you left Niamey, just like Langley's been watching Carl and I. And they're not even…"

"Me," interjected Walid. "It's a direct object, not a subject. Carl and me. And we're all too familiar with Ledeen, creature of Italian so-called intelligence, the bad penny of American imperialism, Mr. "turn the Middle East into a cauldron like I did Central America," and his P2 pals. Billy-gate, Pope-gate, Iran-Contra, ask Allah if there is any scandal they're not in on.

"My ex-CIA friends say their fingerprints were all over that nonsense about Iraq buying our uranium. You remember, Cheney and Rice pushed it to whip up support for Bush's invasion, 'if we wait for a smoking gun it'll be mushroom cloud,' and then the CIA, Congress, and the press rolled over on 'weapons of mass destruction'? As if the French, who run our mining companies, don't know where every gram of uranium goes. As if your wind-sniffing machines didn't know there was no enrichment in Iraq."

"God, you always were a pain in the ass after language training," laughed Jones. "I hate it when people who've learned our language know more about it than we do. And our politics."

"Whatever," Wong cut in. "Save the grammar lessons, and the politics too. What I was saying was, it's not the community I'm most concerned about. It's the other weapons-makers and contactors, our supposed allies in the AIA."

N'Douro looked quizzically at her. "Aerospace Industries Association," she explained. "That's the trade consortium of all the arms exporters. It greases our way in regulations and legislation, somehow carefully dancing around anti-trust laws. Before a deal is signed, it ain't all for one in the AIA, not at all. In fact, it's fair game for other members to block us and poach the deal. That's who I really want to keep in the dark as long as possible."

"Whom. Sorry, Ms. Wong, I'll stop."

"Listen, Walid," Jones cut in, "a deal like this will eventually top a billion dollars, although I think we should just announce the first few years to keep it under that, and stay off the radar. The less anybody knows the better, until we get it past the Pentagon and Congress. And by the way, neither of them are gonna like it, either."

N'Douro seemed surprised by that. "Why would the Air Force oppose aircraft exports? You sell your newest jet fighters to anybody and everybody, to keep your own unit costs down."

"It won't be the Air Force. It'll be the Army. They'll be the ones under the gun, literally, if the AC-130 package ever gets out there to someone who then goes off the reservation. Our top fighters are for sale because only Israel really has the independent command and communication infrastructure and pilot skill needed to fly and fight without our help. And Israel's gonna get whatever we have. Nobody wants to stand in the way of the AIPAC train, especially now, with these anti-Semitic little girls popping up in Congress and giving even minimal scrutiny a bad name. Now, the AC-130s, that's another matter.

"It's easy to fly, just a big cargo plane with simple propeller technology, not computer-aided jets. And a country can always mount the guns with their own ancient computers if we demand they give the new ones back after some incident. That's why the Army has drawn a red line around exporting Puffs. So we've got our work cut out for us. Once the deal is done, we'll be glad to have the AIA in there with us. Their international guy, Kevin Smithson, used to handle arms sales when he was on the staff at Senate Foreign Relations. There's nobody better at quietly slipping a tough sale over the congressional hurdles."

"Well, I still think we've got the upper hand here," said N'Douro. "No Magic Dragons, no base. Tell Langley that and they'll lean on Trump. And the persuasive powers of your congressional leaders with the military factories in their states are legendary. I have a friend, a Saudi general, who got a fleet of the latest M1-A2 tanks because liberal Democratic senators who publicly excoriate the kingdom on human rights and democracy threatened to force the U.S. Army to buy more than they needed with their own budget. And some of them worked with the National Democratic Institute and were on the board of the National Endowment for Democracy, groups that your taxpayers fund to promote democracy around the world!"

The trio sat through a couple more cappuccino breaks, walking through the details of the deal as well-dressed Italian ladies cycled through with hordes of frumpy American and Chinese tourists. Just as they completed their timeline of deliveries, training, and offsets, the outfit of a rare male cappuccino breaker stopped their conversation cold. It was N'Douro who pointed it out. "What is that, an admiral? He looks like Fanucci in Godfather 2, the one with the cape, whom Robert DeNiro shoots to get his start."

"What is it with you men and the Godfather?" groaned Wong. "Can't we go ten minutes without a reference?" They all inspected the gentleman at the bar carefully. He was dressed in a gleaming white suit with military lapels, topped off with a white sailor's cap and a white cape, both trimmed in gold braid. Not just cloth bars but actual medals covered his chest, the full "fruit salad" that officers only wear on formal occasions, like state dinners. He was the center of attention, joking with the ladies on both side of the coffee bar.

"No," said Jones, laughing. "He's no admiral. Look at the shoes: Fratelli

Rossetti tassels for sure. He's a civilian, a bureaucrat with a civil service rank that comes with a uniform. Old European tradition. Gotta love the Italians: above all, *fare una bella figura*."

"All right, last thing," continued N'Douro. "We'd like you to slide in a few other things from other agencies. Nothing linked to the deal, but our *pour lagniappe*. They're your chips— you can give them up in the bargaining if you need to, but the president would be personally grateful to you if you can get them. Because they come from his wives."

N'Douro laid out the ask. The Lion had two wives, one a doctor specializing in tropical medicine and one a mining engineer. Each saw the deal as a chance to boost her favorite project.

The doctor wanted AFRICOM, the U.S. military command, to run a permanent "exercise" with 20 preventive care clinics and 100 clean water sites in the northern areas. She'd watched in frustration as the U.S. development agency, AID, implemented her clinics and wells proposal five years earlier, but with Nigerien personnel and management and a requirement that the Nigerien government take over its funding after two years.

By now all the clinics had closed because the Health ministry couldn't pay the staff, and all the Nigeriens who'd been given medical training had been recruited to Europe's booming nursing homes. All the wells had filled up because the Agriculture ministry didn't have foreign exchange for the spare parts. The doctor concluded it was better to forget "sustainability" and "local buy-in," the AID theories and buzzwords, and just get the Pentagon to maintain the program.

The mining engineer wanted full scholarships to American graduate programs in geology for the top 100 bachelors from the Faculty of Sciences at Abdou Moumouni, the old University of Niamey, and 100 spots for business undergraduates. The graduate students would gradually replace retiring French engineers, and the undergraduate program would cement her support with the urban elites, who would beg her for spots for their children and then back her plans to run for president when Issoufou left office with the $5 million prize.

"Oh, I don't think we'll have to bargain those away," replied Wong. "The universities and their DC lobbying associations would just love to get their hands on qualified black students in the sciences. It helps everybody's diversity targets. Some African-American students, I think it was at Cornell, protested the use of Africans in black diversity statistics, but the backlash put the issue to bed for a while.

"And we can divvy up the undergraduates between the 'land grant' state universities and the black colleges, the HBCUs. Both have killer lobbying arms, and can roll State, Fulbright, or even AID into funding it. And we can make it a public-private partnership, which has been all the rage lately, under both Obama and Trump. We'll make them Boeing-Clyburn scholars, to honor the top African-American in Congress, and nobody will stand in the way. Seems to me, Carl, that Boeing could use some good publicity right about now, with its 737-Max mess."

CHAPTER 4:
FEBRUARY 2020 – THE MURDER

Samuel Solomon cruised in his old Buick down Nannie Helen Burroughs Avenue in Northeast DC. It was a little after five o'clock on a rainy afternoon, and already pitch-black. He was on the second watch, 2:30 in the afternoon to 11 in the evening, but he'd taken a few hours of comp time he'd earned testifying to take his daughter to diving class. Now Solomon—"U" to his family, friends, and colleagues alike from "USS," his nickname in the Navy, day one— was sorry he'd filled in for his wife. It was terrifying to see your teenager skipping around, waving from a slippery rectangle 16 feet in the air above the concrete rim of the pool. He'd mostly covered his eyes and prayed throughout the whole practice.

"U" slowed to avoid an older gentleman who staggered out of the liquor store at 44th, a frayed Cowboys' jersey, number 88, flashing under an open overcoat. Cowboys and Indians, man, that's all we gots down here, Samuel thought. Half of us love Dallas, half of us love the 'Skins. "U" was a Doug Williams man, to the death, but he put the window down and yelled to the guy as he crossed the street: "At least you picked a tight 'Boy. Michael Irvin, the showman! First one to make the No Fun League let the brothers celebrate! Show me the Zorro dance!"

Solomon was on his first tour, a rookie cop on patrol at 42, coming off 20 years in the Navy with a fine Chief Petty Officer's pension for driving those beautiful ships as a helmsman. Policing, he reflected as he watched the old man wander up the block, dancing a sort of jig, was a young person's game. Five years and that would be it. It took a special kind of energy to jump from the mundane to the life-threatening, from lengthy sitting and waiting to wild spurts of action— like when the list of 6-D calls on the cruiser's computer took you from a THFTPROP hanging out there from seven hours ago to a hot-shot ROBARM.

Turning left onto 49th and then right onto Hayes, "U" eased past the Metropolitan Police Department vehicles that were scattered along the median. It was quite a collection: vans, buses, wreckers, pickup trucks, non-transport cruisers, and transport SUVs with the partition grille. There were no parking zone signs here, like there were in the richer parts of town. Nobody would be coming to park here who didn't live here. The only visiting shoppers here waited in their cars for the dealers to come over to them.

An ice cream truck circled the long block, playing an eerie, discordant version of London Bridge. "U" pulled into the barb-wired lot behind the western half of the huge concrete, H-shaped building, where DC's Youth and Family Services was housed. That explained the ice cream truck, looking for little kids attached to mothers and grandmothers who were coming in to plead for lenient treatment for their teenagers.

He presented himself to the camera at the back door of 6-D's eastern side, and was buzzed in. He walked past the reception area where the desk sergeants handled the walk-ins. The glass was bullet-proof and the sergeants wore bullet-proof vests, practices followed since a homicide suspect had stormed into a DC police office and gunned down a detective and two FBI agents. In the hallway there were posters for holiday and retirement parties, and a flyer showing Relisha Rudd, computer-aged to the 14 years old she'd be if she were still alive six years after her disappearance. That was a tribute to her grip on the DC police. There were also four bronze friezes of 6-D cops killed over the last 50 years. That was a tribute too, but also a reminder of what lay out there.

Rachel Craig-Williams was waiting for him in the patrol room, finishing up some computer-work on her kids' dental plan. "Hey 'U'! 'Bout ready to roll? Sarge is asking every damn minute…" Her energy, her youth, her habit, as she often said, of "bringing the extra smile and going the extra mile" in their call-outs, it all reminded him constantly that he was on a five-year clock.

"Peace, partner, for a New York minute." Solomon went into the locker room to change, carrying his belt, which he'd left in the main patrol safe the night before: holster, spray, baton, magazine pouch, flashlight, handcuffs. He already had his gun, the Glock 17, in his coat pocket. It was always, by regulation, in his possession, even off duty.

Craig-Williams was a short, trim woman, just past 30, who'd spent seven years in the Army, using her natural grasp of math to get an accounting degree and become a payroll specialist at DC-area bases. She'd then tried working at the State Department day-care center. The pay was actually OK, enough for raising three children with her mother's help, but she found the work boring, so she moved to MPD. Rachel would never leave the evening shift: it let her see the kids in the morning, feed them, and drive them off to their charter school. Then she stayed on for about an hour, quietly sitting in the back of each of their classrooms before going home for a nap.

At first, the charter didn't know what to do with a mother who said she'd be observing every day. What if other parents and guardians took up the practice, and it became disruptive? But none did, and Rachel never interfered. She just sat there taking notes to discuss with the children the next morning. She'd decided to start observing once she got the evening shift because, having graduated from Anacostia High where you could pass without doing any work, she was determined to have her children ready, as she told them daily, to "get through, not just to" college. Now it was a habit she maintained every day. Her children had long gotten over their embarrassment and were now sort of proud of their diligent mom. They also knew they'd better have their "eyes forward and mouths shut" even when the class was in chaos.

The partners went out to see the shift sergeant, took grief for leaving her short for half a shift, flipped on their body-worn video cameras so they wouldn't have to remember later, and drove their patrol car out into the 6-D. The 6-D cops loved their BWVs, which they simply plugged into a dock for down-loading to the permanent cloud when they came off shift. Citizen complaints had dropped dramatically since the word got out that your tale of police abuse would probably be checkable.

As always, "U" had the wheel because tech-savvy Rachel was so much faster at handling the computer and their cell phones. With the MPD network or the databases it tapped frequently freezing up, the phones were often the quickest way to get and give information.

"Let's see what WALES has got for us," Craig-Williams said as she tapped the mounted keyboard to life. The Washington Area Law Enforcement System immediately displayed lines of 911 calls and assignments, such as DISVER, DISGRP, MENTAL, DRUGUSE, THFTPROP, SHOTFI, ASSTMOTO, STOLENVEH, ASSTOTH, ASLTDV, TRANSPRIS, ROBARM.

DIS was short for disruption, ASST for assist, AS for assault. In addition, real-time audio flowed into the car from commanders and responding cars on various speakers and tactical radios, rising over the soft background music of WPGC (named for black, middle-class Prince George's County, Maryland), which had started to horn in on the "Quiet Storm" programming of Howard University's WHUR.

Their car, 6003E, the "E" being for evening shift, was assigned calls in PSA 602, their primary Public Service Area, of which there were eight in 6-D. There were only two cars out at a time, so they were also often sent to the other PSAs. Their highlighted call was ASSTRES and had been waiting six hours for attention. When they arrived at a tiny, dead-end street, they knew why the residents wanted assistance. A remarkably loud and obnoxious alarm was blaring on a super-sized Ford Expedition SUV, and as soon as the police pulled up people started pouring out of their houses.

First Rachel called for a police wrecker, "the crane," but she was laughed off because of a six-hour backlog. Regulations didn't permit breaking into the van, so she and "U" set about trying to track down the owner. For an hour they called other MPD districts and a few Maryland departments and sent computer queries to MPD's COBALT database. Rachel also tried five other regional systems and a new federally-funded anti-terrorism intelligence system she'd never heard of before it was suggested by a dispatcher in 5-D, where the SUV's owner was listed as a landlord. She finally got a contact number for him from the record of a 911 call he'd made in Baltimore three years earlier about his Yorkie puppy being stolen from his house.

The residents of the street kept thanking the pair for their tenacity, and Rachel kept giving them back her mantra, "extra smiles and extra miles—

we work for you." And then, before she could even make the call, the owner simply showed up, by chance. He'd parked his van there before going to his construction job in a part of town that did have parking restrictions. "No need to write this into COBRA," the dispatcher relayed for the sergeant. The partners groaned on hearing this. It was her little way of punishing them for "U" taking time off: their evaluation statistics wouldn't show any productivity for the first hour.

A couple of hours more of armed social work followed. First "U" and Rachel took an ASSTPERS, accompanying EMTs who revived an obese man who'd passed out while cooking for his family. Then they caught a DESPROP, which ended up in a drug arrest of probably the only white prostitute walking east of the river— a wasted, acne-scarred woman who'd bizarrely reported herself for smashing the windshield of her pimp's camper outside a gas station on Kenilworth Avenue, the highway to Baltimore.

She carried no ID, but the name she gave popped up on bench warrants in the District and South Carolina. They figured she just wanted shelter from the nasty weather and maybe a medically-monitored break from the crack pipe she told them was in her jeans pocket. The woman was so skinny, having lost her appetite to the drugs, that she had to hold her pants up with her fingers in the loops when Rachel went into the front pockets to get the pipe and the rock.

The arrest was difficult, since the prostitute alternated between elegant politeness and animalistic anger. She suddenly spit and shrieked out every vile name she could at Rachel, and demanded to be searched only by "U". So they had to cuff her for the search, which had to be made by a woman if one was present. But the partners stayed calm and talked to her quietly, and after the transport SUV with the grille came for her, they high-fived each other: "That's our night!" It was only 8, but they knew it would take two hours of paperwork, minimum, to process the arrest back at 6-D. They were going off the board, having "stayed safe" for another shift.

But as they pulled away, everything changed, as it always could. Dispatch didn't bother with the WALES listing for this one. All Tac channels were overridden: "MAC-10, shots fired, ASVIC, ASVIC, Benning Heights, 46 and F Southeast. PSA 604. All units 6-D, 7-D." Rachel flipped the siren and they screamed off to Simple City, a mile to the south, knowing they might well be outgunned while "assisting the victim" until SWAT made the scene from downtown. It's illegal to covert a machine gun to full auto, but when your gun is already illegal, who cares?

* * *

Black got the call from her grandmother at 9 p.m. The thieves had taken Du'Shaunn's fancy new Jackie Robinson team jacket but left his wallet and ID in his pocket. Residents watching the crime scene had told the homicide detectives from downtown, La'Damien Cass and Shirley Tono, where he lived on the Ridge. By 9:30 Black was at the perimeter, flashing her FBI creds and telling "U" and Rachel, who had the clipboards at the east end of the taped-off ball field, to either let her through or bring the detectives over.

Mary Olive had been calm and measured: "The 5-0 say Du'Shaunn been shot dead, probably for that got-damn jacket I told him not to buy. Up by the Rec Center. Don't come see me 'til you Gat the punks." Black wasn't going to shoot anybody, but she was going to make sure the killers went to jail.

At this first meeting the detectives didn't inspire much confidence in her. The tall, black, muscular guy, Cass, never said a word, and let the rotund white woman, Tono, handle Black's questions. She treated her like a grieving relative, not an FBI agent, deflecting her questions about evidence, motives, and leads. They didn't even ask her what she knew about Du'Shaunn, his habits, or his friends. They were blowing her off, and having paid due courtesy to both her family connection and her creds, they were anxious to get back to the murder site and keep poking around for evidence.

"Well, are you canvassing yet, can you give me some doors to handle? If you're not gonna bother to learn about 'Shaunn from me, at least don't let these hours slip, when crimes get solved or not!" Black was starting to get hot, falling back on her old gangster ways in her first confrontation in Simple City since she left for the Army. The detectives were used to relatives' emotions, and soft-shoed her. Cass spoke up, quietly, for the first time.

"Look, Agent McGurk, this is a shit time, but it's our shit time. We close 'em, you feel me? It's not like a Harry Bosch novel or an FBI training manual down here. The first hour theory is bullshit for us. Nobody talks to the cops when the killers are watching. That's a death warrant. We solve most of our east of the river cases, but our breaks can come months after the fact, when a banger needs to snitch his way out of another mess. Let us do our job here, and if your grandmother agrees, we'll treat you as the family rep, and brief you every week. And you can bet we'll be by to question everybody who knew your cousin, you included. But our cases are usually marathons, not sprints. It's not gonna happen tonight. Now, we gotta go back and look for the brass. You go see your family. Help them."

Black backed down, nodding her head and biting her tongue, certain that Cass and Tono knew full well that "brass" in cop-slang also included steel shell casings, like those on some MAC-10 "Parabellum" bullets. "OK, I got it. But just remember, you need to jump the line at the labs, you need to use FBI goodies, you call me. Nobody gettin' in my way there— and I got a lot of favors to call in."

Within the month, she had a much better opinion of Cass and Tono. And they had a much better opinion of her. The detectives had built an impressive profile of Du'Shaunn and his last week alive, and had in fact leaned on her to run a search on his Jackie Robinson jacket. She added it to her list of requests at Public Corruption on yet another Providence mayor's bribery case, and what came back in two days, with typical, over-staffed FBI speed, put the detectives in her debt.

It was common practice for take-off artists to trade sports shoes, shirts, caps, and jackets with other thieves. That way they had swag and a reputation, but no connection to that particular crime if a victim told the police he'd seen somebody wearing their property: "Bought it off some guy I saw downtown. Nah, I don't remember where, maybe up on 14th and U. Nah, don't remember him, never saw him before. What day was it stolen? I was at my aunt's house in South Carolina that whole weekend. You can check."

Since thieves removed all the stickers and tags that black kids usually left on their clothes as a fashion statement, it was even hard to prove that the item was the same one that was stolen. But with the FBI research, Cass and Tono had a few aces in the hole. The Bureau geeks had found from social media pictures of Du'Shaunn that his jacket was a rare variant, made not by a large clothing company but by a politically-conscious start-up of two

"Aggies"— graduates of the storied HBCU, North Carolina Agricultural and Technical.

They were Engineering majors, with Black History minors, who had first designed the jackets for their fraternity "step" team, to honor black heroes and institutions. So the front didn't even read "Brooklyn Dodgers," but instead had the big K C logo of the Kansas City Monarchs, the Negro League team Robinson played for before Branch Rickey spirited him away. And there was no 42 superimposed over his image across the back, but 5, his Monarchs' number.

For every production run of 100 jackets the company stitched a different black hero's name next to Jackie's on the sleeves, somebody with a connection to his life. Du'Shaunn's jacket, Mary Olive recalled, featured Paul Robeson, a noted civil rights figure Robinson had been called to denounce as a Communist at a 1949 House Un-American Activities Committee hearing on "Communist Infiltration of Minority Groups." But he sand-bagged the Committee, testifying that "Negroes were stirred up long before there was a Communist Party, and they'll stay stirred up long after the party has disappeared, unless Jim Crow has disappeared by then as well."

Cass and Tono had asked the MPD officers who worked inside the three public high schools east of the river to look out for the jacket. At least half of the high school students east of the river were in its 12 charters schools, so the second-shift sergeants in 6-D and 7-D gave them a week of patrols to watch those at dismissal. Of course, at least a third of the teenagers in that area had already dropped out, and the jacket might have been traded in another part of the city, or in Prince George's County, so the detectives put out bulletins and themselves drove the streets and looked in on the projects. It took a few days, because most students attended irregularly, but they soon had a patrol report on a boy who'd been seen coming out of the Friendship School on Minnesota Avenue, wearing this particular version of the jacket.

As requested, the patrol officers didn't approach the boy, but simply followed him and called Cass and Tono. To spook him they'd decided to skip the usual questioning and simply arrest him on the spot for theft during a homicide. That automatically put the boy on a "no-bail" in the DC Jail's wing for teenagers being tried as adults. As they expected, within two days his court-appointed attorney came to them with a trade: the name of the boy with whom he'd traded jackets, in return for all charges being dropped. The detectives said they'd keep his name confidential and that he probably would never have be called to testify. Just to be safe, though, his aunt that very day sent the snitch to live with relatives in Florida, to avoid the ditches in DC.

To Black's surprise, Cass and Tono already had the kid he'd fingered, a 17-year-old HD drop-out named Tupelo Jones, on a list of suspected members of the Clay Kings. Clay Terrace was a tough patch of public housing on a ridge that looked down on HD from the south. Tono laid it out for Black. "The dean of students, the enforcer, really, at HD told us that Du'Shaunn had punched a boy named La'Darius Ennis to the ground in a cafeteria fight, just a week before he was killed. We went to Gangs— oh, sorry, we now have to say CIU, Criminal Interdiction Unit— and got a list of the Kings. Ennis was on it: he ran for them, got caught, didn't snitch, went to Juvie for them two years ago, when he was 14. And get this, our boy Tupelo Jones was on there too. He's more of a player than Ennis— same age, but he left school at 16 to handle Kings business."

Black knew that the sets used kids under 16 to deliver all their drugs, because they couldn't be tried as adults, but only as PINs— Persons in Need of Supervision. She knew because she'd been a runner herself. She also knew that by law kids in DC couldn't drop out until they were 18, but that there weren't enough truant officers and cops in the world to make that stick. In the rare case they could find a parent or more typically a guardian to complain, they were more likely to get lies than cooperation.

"So, Mar'Shae, this changes things," explained Tono. "We think this was payback, not a robbery. The Kings probably figured they had to back up their boy Ennis to keep their cred, so they sent a crew off to do it. Jones was probably in the crew. The jacket turned out to be a bonus they couldn't pass up.

"This is the break we needed, but it may take a while. We can't charge Jones based on the teen's information. He might know something about it, but we can't put him at the scene based on a jacket he can claim he got from somebody else. That's just not solid enough for a warrant to tear apart his house and his life. Jones'll know that too, so we can't even sweat him. Hell, if we spook him now, he may disappear into the Carolina mist."

Black pushed back: "Are you kidding? Wait while the case is hot, because he might try to hide? If the FBI was doing this, we'd bring in Jones and everybody who ever had the slightest contact with him, and just ruin their lives, seize everything until we got answers. And if somebody ran, you can be damned sure we'd find him."

"Peace, blood," Cass laughed. "You keep forgetting it's not an FBI case. We have to use the tools we have. Listen up. We ask CIU to watch Jones and take him when he screws up, which in his line of work won't be long. Any drug charge'll do it, even marijuana if he's on Park Service or other federal land, which isn't subject to DC's 'recreational use' exception. He's already on juvie probation for a gun ticket, so we get the prosecutors to hold hard on drugs or any bullshit charge, even associating with another felon, and he knows he can go away for ten.

"Then we give him one chance to give us an up-close and personal on how the shooting went down, and who the shot-caller was, for a lighter sentence on the murder. The first guy to fold is the one who can spin a story of just being there, and not touching the gun.

"That's SOP for us— we'll never know who did what in the planning and the shooting of your cousin anyway, so it makes no difference who agrees to be our witness. We clear the case, since somebody goes down full-time. When we bring a bunch of guys in for deadly assault or murder, somebody always snitches. Jones'll be glad to be the first one out of the box. Out in three beats out in 20, period. It's so obvious that we don't even offer witness protection. Of course, the snitch has to give up the shot-caller too. But they rarely go down, because I guarantee you the prosecutor will let the shot-caller trade in whatever scumbag rented him the guns."

Black was puzzled. "Rent? Why rent a MAC, when every little rascal is carrying a popper?"

Cass jumped in. "You're behind the times, sugar. Lots of sets don't have their own Gats anymore, like when you were coming up. Ratting on a gun has become too sweet a get-out-of-jail-free card. Instead of risking getting sold out and caught with one, the bangers rent them, by the hour, through as many as two or three cut-outs. And they give them back when the hour is up. We break beaucoup cases where we get a witness on the shooter because he couldn't afford to wait until the Vic was alone— he had to get the Gat back before the next hour chimed! It's like Captain Ahab and Moby Dick when prosecutors sniff a renter. Immediate hard-on: that's a career case."

The Melville reference went right over Black's head, but she didn't bother asking. Her mind jumped instead to a different classic. *Vengeance is mine, I will repay, saith the Lord.* The one structured time in her childhood had been Mary Olive's Sunday morning readings from the New Testament, and she remembered that line from the letter to the Romans by the guy who became Paul on the road to Damascus. Well, it looked like the Lord was gonna give Mary Olive some satisfaction.

PART II:
THE CHASE

CHAPTER 5:
MARCH 2020 – WHISTLEBLOWERS

It was a quiet Tuesday in the Washington offices of World Financial Transparency, a non-profit research center focused on reducing corruption in international business. WFT analyzed and publicized Treasury Department compilations of Suspicious Activities Reports. Its calling card was its own on-line, country-by-country database of invoices that governments and auditors had to publish under a variety of international agreements. WFT's model left it to others, particularly governments, to investigate the invoices that it highlighted as worthy of review. WFT didn't have the staff resources for that, and in any case its mission from its founding ten years before had always been to help governments set up transparent systems, rather than to solve particular crimes.

WFT director Mary Magdalen Carter worked her way through the mail on her desk. Soon she came to a bulky FedEx envelope from Niamey, Niger. The "sender" area was blank. Inside she found a stack of financial computer runs with highlights and written notes alongside them, all in French. The final sheet was a hand-written note, in rough English, on the letterhead of the Nigerien Ministry of Finance.

"Regard you same invoices in the database Niger of you. More half to the Delaware."

Carter didn't speak French, but after three decades in the DC human rights world, she knew people she could trust who did. She called Pierre

Nkumbo, a friend who ran the Africa Division of Human Rights Watch, and asked him to come by when he had time. While WFT paid for jammers and a weekly anti-bugging sweep, she thought that nothing good could come from telling Nkumbo on the phone why she wanted to see him. She'd also instituted physical security when she'd taken the job at WFT three years before, like coded doors and a bullet-proof guard area. Amnesty International and other groups who criticized foreign officials by name had long needed this sort of protection from enraged relatives and landsmen living in the States. Threatening people's money seemed to her as dangerous as threatening their official positions.

When Nkumbo came by that afternoon Carter took the FedEx envelope out of her safe and asked him to give it a good read, comparing the highlighted transactions to the Niger entries she'd printed out from the WFT database. Knowing the first question HRW's fundraisers would want him to ask, she said: "Of course, anything we do with this, you guys can have a piece. But first tell me what the hell it is."

Sitting at WFT's conference table in silence for two hours, Nkumbo took copious notes, switching back and forth between the Nigerien and WFT printouts. Then he called Carter into the room and shut the door. "How secure are we to talk here? Because this is a nuclear bomb that could do Boeing more harm than the 737-Max, and Mobe-Corp more harm than their shoot-up in Afghanistan. And where there's Mobe-Corp, there's the CIA, since they help each other, both in operations and banking.

"Remember the BCCI bank scandal, in the '80s? Big money, the spooks, they don't just sit there and take it. They snoop, they leak, and they definitely try to kill the messengers— well, not kill, I don't think, but destroy the reputations of the whistleblowers and their advocates. This is dangerous stuff, for us personally and I'm sure for our groups. I'll kick it up our chain of command, orally, confidentially, but my bet is we won't want any part of the lead on this. We don't really do corruption, directly, just like we don't do democracy. Soros always insisted that we'd have more credibility and broader funding if we stuck just to human rights.

"I do think we'd probably join some coalition you put together from the groups that oppose AFRICOM, once it's big and rolling. And that's better than you'll get from Amnesty— their London lawyers will rule this outside their mandate, period, like they did the 'no arms to dictators' stuff because nobody's been tortured with a tank— it just keeps them in power so they can torture with a knife. This is really more Center for International Policy stuff anyway. You know, Don Ranard, Bob White, Bill Goodfellow, rock and roll and name names. They always had the *huevos*. Hey, Salih Booker took over for Bubblin' Bill, so he'd be giving you the AFRICOM connections and the Nigerien politics, and Bill Hartung does all their arms trade stuff. They'd eat this up."

"Good Lord," Carter chuckled, "an NGO passing up publicity and fund-raising, giving it all to somebody else? I've never heard of that, so this must be top shelf— tell me."

"*Bien*, the bottom line is that an enterprising auditor at the Ministry didn't stop with just recording the invoices from the explosion of Boeing and Mobe-Corp deals in Niger after the big gunship sale last year. That's all here, the servicing contracts as well as the payments for local construction and consulting from the offsets Niger demanded as part of the gunship agreement. No, whoever leaked this went off on their own and matched up Treasury SARs and your international database, triangulating to find dollars on the American side that should have been on the CFA invoices in Niger, but weren't. And about 300 million of it is missing, about half of the total, like the note says. That's from about 400 separate invoices, all deposited in Delaware corporate accounts.

"But here's the *pièce de résistance:* They've written names, Nigerien and American, for about 20 of the invoices that match specific Delaware deposits. That's the bomb. They've already found some of the Nigerien names on London and New York real estate buys, within two months of the over-invoicing. I remember you guys did a report on that as a good way to launder dirty money. Make a cash offer over the list price to make a quick deal, right?"

After Nkumbo left, Carter called in her senior staff and got her board chair to come over from his law firm. This was the big one, the one that could make WFT's bones. After this, it wouldn't be them constantly courting the media and the congressional committees, but the other way around. If WFT said that their main legislative fix, Maxine Waters' bill to require states to reveal the names of the beneficial owners to the feds, was a litmus test on money-laundering, then it would be, and it would move. A call to the Treasury wouldn't end up with a congressional relations pipsqueak, but the relevant assistant secretary. And banks and brokers would signal their virtue by funding WTF, just like oil companies did with "climate change" groups.

But taking Canned Heat's advice to her at Woodstock, Carter wasn't going down "this long and lonesome road all by myself." The road would get rocky, as another of her favorites had sung while inventing bluegrass, and she wanted everybody locked in from the start. She ran through Nkumbo's take for the staff and the chair, swore them to secrecy from spouse and friends, and then added: "If Treasury had this material, they could solve these cases in about five minutes, and if they get the signature files from the Nigerien finance office, they could prosecute them in about ten. Those names are going to be top Nigerien officials, or more likely their relatives, and top Boeing and Mobe-Corp executives. Our choice here is to give it all to Treasury, and threaten to publish in six months if nothing happens, or publish now, working with CIP, and make it happen."

Carter knew what her choice would be, but she wanted the Board to take the weight. After a lengthy discussion with the senior staff, the chair spent the rest of the day on the secure phone at his firm, talking with the board and the lawyers. The decision was unanimous: bring in the Center for International Policy and publish the "FedEx Files," as they were already calling them, with an exclusive at the Times, Post, or Journal, and then get out of the way while the relevant congressional committees and the wall-to-wall liberal cable pundits screamed for Treasury to take them up and run.

Not a month later Mar'Shae McGurk received an email from her boss in Public Corruption:

"Black, what we talked about is now official. Pass Providence on to Johnson and Gunnell and brief them as needed. You're now the AIC, lead on the FedEx Files. I'll give you two agents from our international group and two from military contracting. Just let me know who you want. Then work with Legal on the mandate and send it to me for editing. Go as high as you can at both corporations with immunity and pleas, you know the drill, and Justice can try the last man or woman standing."

* * *

"I can teach you a lot better, and you can learn a lot more from each other, if we all know something about the skills and experiences your colleagues bring to this class. Let's create a list of variables, like where you're from, your artistic or athletic interests, political orientation, what you like to do, what your parents do for a living, where you've traveled, what identities are important to you, ethnic, religious, or sporting, from the Nation of Islam to Red Sox nation. After we have that you can put in your answers, and present them today in class, maybe a two-minute summary. Then hand them in to me so I can spend my weekend seeing just what in the world I'm dealing with here!"

Two months before the FedEx package landed at WFT, LaKisha Blunt was in the first meeting of her Civilizations of Africa class of 30 undergraduates in American University's School of International Service. She was in her second year of a non-tenure but full-time assistant professorship. It had a five-year limit that had been negotiated with the national association of university professors. Technically, it was an annual contract, but it always ran to the limit, her colleagues told her.

Six courses a year and $75,000! Professor Blunt was enjoying the pay and health insurance while she could, knowing that after this she'd go back to the adjunct ranks, running around course-to-course at local four-year and community colleges at about $3,000 per class, a quarter of her current rate, and buying her own Obamacare. Her father had been a professor at Hampton in the old days, when every teacher on campus was on the tenure track. Now it was down to a quarter nationally, with temps and adjuncts picking up the rest. A new business model. Where did all that tuition money go?

Blunt had tried womanfully not to be an Africanist. All her non-black mentors had expected her to be one, and all her black mentors had told her not to. Condi Rice, who spoke at her Spelman graduation before she went to Tufts' Fletcher School for her Ph.D., took her aside and recounted how studying Russia had made her career. "If it had been a room full of Africanists at Stanford, Brent Scowcroft wouldn't have noticed me. But it was the Soviet crowd, talking arms control, and I was a burning black light!"

But Africa, its history and people, turned out to be what Blunt loved. Her mentors, of all ethnic groups, had said if you didn't love the topic, you couldn't get through a dissertation, let alone spend the rest of your career on dissertation-style work. You needed some heavy motivation for a life of lonely devotion to impossible completeness in research and unattainable perfection in writing something that nobody but you ever really reads.

As a graduate student Blunt has enjoyed her required survey courses in different regions of the world, but the African peoples and their promise had hooked her from the very first scene in the very first episode of a PBS series she was assigned to watch. Ali Mazrui's The Africans explored the "triple heritage" of Western, Islamic, and traditional influences on African culture, politics, economics, and religion. The notion of an entire continent seized and then "pushed to the very periphery of world affairs" intrigued her.

An afternoon in the library stacks, pulling books on underdevelopment and poverty, sealed the deal. Powerful kingdoms, a God's treasure chest of resources, colonial devastation, neo-colonialism in its aftermath, and now the world's lowest levels of electricity, clean water, income, and life expectancy— it felt to Blunt like Africa was the one place in the world where the fundamental story of the transition to modernity wasn't over. She wrote her dissertation while living in Kenya on a fellowship and interviewing Somali refugees. Her topic was the disintegration of Somalia after U.S. military intervention. Not George Bush's well-publicized armed delivery of relief supplies in 1992 that led to "mission creep" and Black Hawk down under Bill Clinton, but Jimmy Carter's original decision in 1979 to arm the Marxist dictator in his civil war in return for military bases for a U.S. Rapid Deployment Force in the Middle East.

Blunt's undergraduates responded energetically and with humor, as she had hoped, to the chance to present themselves to their peers. For her, though, the real benefit wasn't that they'd had to buy in from the beginning to the idea that they should contribute to the class, but the information she had on every student. Now she could tailor her remarks to have a reason to put them on the spot: "Well, let's ask our Irish-American friend, whose ancestors formed the bulk of the British troops marching to seize the Golden Stool of the Ashanti, to describe that campaign to us next class…let's ask the rugby player if she'd be willing to tell us the tale next time of Mandela and the first World Championship after apartheid."

Looking over the submissions from the class later that day, Blunt notice something strange. There were six foreign students out of the 30, which was typical, but five were from one country, which was not. And it was a small country, Niger. They were also all in the Business school, which was even stranger. She'd only had one business undergraduate in an Africa course in two years. Rereading their submissions, she saw they all had fathers who were high government officials or owners of successful companies.

Blunt was used to her foreign students, particularly Chinese, Saudi, and UAEs, being from wealthy families. Like most universities, and even some private high schools, AU had long promoted itself to those families, who paid cash on the barrelhead at the rarely-used listed tuition. It was a global phenomenon, with top British and South African universities also relying on foreign cash to feed their state-starved institutions. Even state universities in America had a version, recruiting out-of-state students who paid a far higher tuition. But this concentration of Nigeriens seemed different to Blunt.

A call to a friend who worked in the International Students office revealed that all the Nigeriens had come to AU on a scholarship program paid for by AID, the U.S. Agency for International Development. Why, Blunt wondered, would wealthy students be given money by an anti-poverty program that had been under budget pressure from the day Trump took office? It didn't take much internet digging, just a skim through AID's on-line congressional presentations and a few stories on Niger's new status as AFRICOM's airfield in West Africa, for her to get the picture. Her students' parents were the powerful allies of one of the president's wives in her bid to replace her husband. AID's anti-poverty money was sweetening an arms deal. And it pissed her off that she was part of the plot.

The professor's first mistake was to expect her dean to be upset too. A decade before, SIS had received bad publicity during the fundraising for its new "Green" building by taking money from a Bahraini prince and a Nigerian politician. One had been a leader in a feudal Sunni government whose troops had fired on pro-democracy demonstrators from the Shia majority, using U.S. guns that had been a Somali-like payoff for being the base for the U.S. 7th fleet. The other was accused of corruption and money-laundering after an investigation by a Senate Committee. It became clear to her in their meeting that the last thing the dean wanted was to do was dig under this Nigerien rock.

The professor's second mistake was to respond to the dean's dismissal of her concerns by writing a piece about the AID program and its link to the arms deal in the student newspaper, the Eagle. By serendipity it came out just as the FedEx story broke, and Human Rights Watch and other organizations in the left-leaning Africa Working Group were trying to decide what to do about a request from WFT and CIP to join them in a lobbying campaign.

The goal of the campaign was to put into the annual foreign aid appropriation a prohibition on further funding of the Niger deal, until the administration "certified that all offset arrangements in Niger have been credibly investigated and potential crimes properly prosecuted, both in Niger and the United States." This sort of half-way measure was a "bridge vote" that the groups hoped Members could eventually walk all the way over to their true goal of an outright ban on arms sales to Africa.

Blunt's revelations were picked up by the Chronicle of Higher Education and then by the New York Times as part of continued coverage of its exclusive on the FedEx Files. As a result, not only did the African advocacy groups, mostly religious and development lobbies, decide to sign onto the campaign, but university and other policy groups promoting international education did so as well. By the end of the semester, Blunt was informed that she wouldn't be renewed for the next year. Nothing to do with her article, of course; just an influx of new tenure-track hires who would have priority for the Africa courses. She was offered an appointment as an adjunct, but was warned that there would be at most one course available in the coming year.

CHAPTER 6:
MAY 2020 – INVESTIGATIONS

"The *** State Department desk officers here in DC talk to the *** embassy people in Niger, and the *** embassy people in Niger talk to the *** CIA. Now, you can never tell anything, really, in that 'wilderness of mirrors,' but I'm pretty sure the CIA uses Mobe-Corp all over the world and wants to keep that going. So essentially, Agent McGurk, you are working against most of our own government. If you want to crack this case, you reveal nothing to the desk officers and I reveal nothing to the embassy people.

"And that goes double for the ATA, the 'anti-terrorism' trainers from State. They're just cops training cops, which was supposed to have ended in the '70s, for Christ's sake, and there is no such thing as a straight cop in West Africa. I was there for ten years, and I can tell you they all put tribal loyalties above their government mission. Nothing stays secret.

"To be African is to be part of a tribal nation, in everything you do, and the boundaries of the nations have nothing to do with the boundaries the Europeans drew for the countries. So nearly every African country contains a number of nations, fighting for supremacy out of self-protection. Anything resembling a fair election is really just a census, with everybody voting for their tribal party. It sort of turns Clausewitz's dictum on its head: politics there is a continuation of war by other means."

Black was in the office of Charles Hilliard Burr III, "Trey" to one and all, the head of the FBI's International Operations Division. She'd never heard of Clausewitz, or a dictum, but she was used by now to keeping a straight face when hearing what other people considered common references. And she was planning to freeze out all the other agencies anyway. Until ordered differently, that's what FBI agents always did.

Except for his South "Bahston" accent and tough guy cursing, Trey seemed to be lifted from the Brooks Brothers catalogues she used for her shirts— white, tall, athletic, and slender even in his '60s, with the perfect light tan and a lot of elegantly groomed hair. He ran 63 "legats," overseas offices staffed with FBI legal attachés. The regional office covering Niger was in Abuja, the constructed capital of Nigeria, and Black was preparing to fly there to direct the search for the Nigeriens named in the FedEx Files.

"Fine, I'll follow the legat's lead, but if tribal politics is everything, I need to know about that. And if I can't use State, I'll need some other experts to bring me up to speed. Who should that be?"

"Probably somebody French," replied Burr. "I don't know who you could trust not to rat you out to the SE, which would certainly leak it back to Langley. But Terry Crawford-Browne would, from his network of international bankers he built for the anti-apartheid movement, and you need to talk with him anyway. I mean for hours— which he is always happy to give.

"He's the man on arms trade corruption, lives in Cape Town, and seems to live a charmed existence. Maybe it's the aura of his wife's old boss, Archbishop Tutu, maybe it's his great press connections, but nobody's silenced him yet, from his days as a banker, leading the South African sanctions fight from within, to his days as the scourge of his old pals in the ANC, when they brokered the massive arms deal 25 years ago, under Mandela's government, that got them all rich. Terry had the financial chops to decipher all that and lay it out on a platter for the press. Of course, the government just labels him a kook and tries to pretend he had nothing to do with the liberation."

Black knew what apartheid referred to, but "ANC" and "Tutu" were new to her. To cover her gaps with this preppy she turned to something she did know, her grandmother's Gospel readings. "A prophet is not without honor, but in his own country," she quoted, "but why should I trust him? He sounds like those folks at WFT, getting famous by publishing everything about FedEx on the web but not caring that the cockroaches started scrambling for the dark before I could even get started." Black had just come from a singularly unproductive interview with Mary Magdalen Carter, the boss at WFT, who kept saying that everything she had was out there for all to see, and that she had nothing to add.

"McGurk, take a step back and think about it. Crawford-Browne and WFT did the same thing, for the same reason. Reporting a politically-sensitive crime to a government rather than the media means that, at best, it's pursued quietly until it hits a low wall and stops. I'm sure those Weathermen in your last case had a lot to say about the My Lai massacre. Well, if the grunts who reported it to the Army in '68 had instead gone straight to Sy Hersh, the Army could never have gotten out of it with just one lieutenant serving three years of house arrest. Did you know that American hero Colin Powell was a young major on the general staff in that division, assigned to investigate a soldier's claim of witnessing atrocities, and he never even interviewed the soldier?

"In the case of South Africa's arms deal, not just the ANC, but France, the UK, and Germany, those great transparent democracies, covered up the bribes in every way they could. Britain's prime minister, Tony Blair, even formally invoked national security to shut down his own governments' investigators, people like us, in a related case of arms bribery in Saudi Arabia. Meanwhile the so-called South African navy doesn't dare submerge its German submarines, which they have no use for anyway, and still aren't paid off.

"Without Terry going public, nobody would ever have known about the billions in bogus offsets and straight-up cash. Now, what makes you think the same sort of cover-up wouldn't have happened here, if WFT had just forwarded the files to Treasury? Frankly, I think it strengthens your hand in pushing this, to have the FedEx Files out in public."

So Black connected with Crawford-Browne, via Skype. She'd found him in Berlin, where he was the main speaker at a demonstration against RheinMetall, a German arms-maker that owned the munitions branch of the South African Denel parastatal. The protestors were calling for an end to exports by both companies to Saudi Arabia, which had been bombing Yemen with their merchandise.

The veteran campaigner gave her hours of detail on the ways the flood of European cash had been routed through offsets and off-shore accounts to the ANC officials who approved various part of the first big arms deal after liberation. He just kept on, adding juicy levels of detail to every new topic the previous one suggested. Twice Black had to leave one of her agents at the screen and duck out to use the bathroom.

When she told Crawford-Browne she thought she had enough material to start with, he turned to a new topic, warning her how hard and dangerous it was to get governments to investigate their own corruption when weapons and the ever-attendant flow of bribes were involved. There'd been a number of unsolved murders that disrupted the Arms Deal investigations, he said, and the charges he'd made were just now coming to trial, after two decades of government resistance.

Burr's guess had been right: Crawford-Browne's network of contacts included some French banking colleagues who'd worked in Niger. Black's agents managed to track a few of them down, and arranged for her to interview them in Paris and Aix-en-Provence before flying into Abuja from London.

Echoing something Crawford-Browne had told her about Africa's trade patterns 60 years after independence, the travel office told Black that after working in Abuja for a week she and the legat team would have to fly back to London to get to Niamey. Apparently, most flights into Africa's major cities still followed colonial routes. The surest, safest, and probably even quickest way to travel the 600 miles from Abuja to Niamey was actually 6,000 miles: British Airways nonstop to London, take the Chunnel train over to Paris, and fly Air France nonstop to the Nigerien capital. And that was the route Black and her team traveled in July after two weeks of digging through the regional databases in the Abuja office. They planned to spend at least a month in Niamey.

On the same May day she met Trey Burr, Black headed out in the late afternoon to meet up with the DC homicide detectives handling Du'Shaunn's case, La'Damien Cass and Shirley Tono. Their working relationship was tight now, and when the understaffed DC crime lab had been unable after three months to find any match for the shell casings at the scene, they took her up on her offer to jump the line at the FBI national crime lab in Quantico. That lab had a lot more databases than DC, and a lot better and a lot bigger bunch of computers and programmers.

Black got the name and cell number of a black gun tech at Quantico from her old boss in Cold Case, Jerry Cummings, and asked her for the favor, without paper, with nothing written out, not even a text or email. To keep the case file pure, Cass and Tono would guide the DC lab to the right database if Quantico got a hit.

It took the gun tech all of five minutes to find a match in a shooting in Alexandria, the Virginia city that had originally been part of the District of Columbia. It hadn't made it into the regional assault on persons database that MPD used, because the shooter had fired against a wall to encourage the Vic's cooperation during a robbery. But the Justice Department's Bureau of Alcohol, Tobacco, Firearms, and Explosives (still known just as ATF from its roots in the Treasury Department "revenuers" and Eliot Ness' "Untouchables") systematically collected information on every shot fired in every crime, and Quantico had access to that database.

Black met the detectives at the Arlington County jail, where Jerome Cleaveland was serving a 14-month sentence for the robbery. "Who is he?" she asked them. "DC low-life, a gang-banger without a gang, 20, out of Northwest, no connection east of the river," answered Cass, "caught by a garage camera but didn't have the gun when he was arrested. He was offered a pass if he gave up a renter, but he wouldn't even admit he'd used one. He ended up actually lecturing the judge with that tired old 'snitches get stitches and end up in ditches' when he was given one last chance at sentencing. Pled to robbery three with jail, not prison. Has a couple of kids, a couple of Juvie street robberies without a weapon, no job, ever, not even in that summer program where all you have to do is sign up, not show up."

"Look," interjected Tono, "two shootings, within two months, same gun, 15 miles apart, one by a gang and one by a lone stick-up artist. You know that screams 'renter.' Let's see if we can use you, McGurk, to push him, put the FBI fear into him."

So they agreed on a play and went into a certified-unrecorded room to talk with Cleaveland and his lawyer. For a robbery case, he hadn't even merited a public defender, so he'd been assigned one of the young attorneys that judges could call for a flat, and low, fee. Cleaveland was a large young man, slow-moving and clearly comfortable around legal personnel. He didn't look too intimidated as Black laid out the link to a murder and the FBI's interest in it.

Before his lawyer could open her mouth, Cleaveland took over. "Homie," he said to Black, "you not straight up. Don't know why you here, but you ain't here as FBI— they comes in pairs and threes, Word. Now you say you can get the judge to redo my sentence based on non-coöp on the 1-8-7, but I knows it ain't so. Start breakin' deals and nobody pleads in Arlington County again, ever. How's this jail gonna look then? How they gonna fill all those juries, then, when perps all demand 'em? I took this meet 'cause maybe you had something for me, but I got nothing for you. Sure, I used a renter, but like I told the judge, snitches…"

"That's all, detectives," cut in the lawyer. "And remember, my client ran his mouth without my approval, but you guys and I agreed that this was informal. I don't want any of this written down."

"Damn," said Black, as they walked out to their cars. "What're you gonna do now?"

"Ah, don't fret, sister" replied Cass. "We didn't expect much there from your 'homie,' but now we know to work the renter angle, for sure. We don't have any breaks yet with the jacket-trader, Tupelo Jones, so we need to start working suspected Clay Kings shot-callers. No warrants but lots of gang unit, ah, CIU, surveillance. Again, we find anything illegal, we hammer them. Don't worry— something will break. We're gettin' there."

Black didn't tell the detectives, but she had her own ideas about finding the Clay Kings' shot-caller. It had been her neighborhood and never theirs. She had her old girls, she had her extended family, and she could ask them what they already knew and ask them to keep their ears open and their mouths shut. There was no need to warn them of the dangers of the Kings getting wind of their interest— they knew the game. She was back in her world, but not as an FBI agent. Yeah, that was one of the last things 'Shaunn ever said to her: "Black is back!" Oh yeah, she thought, you damn skippy.

Black had two jobs now. Every evening after work she'd walk Benning Heights, tracking down her old girls from 15 years before, one by one. A few were around, a few were dead, and one, La Shonda, the math wiz who kept all their accounts perfectly in her head, was halfway across the country in a max for doing the same thing, it turned out, for the Clay Kings. Black immediately took the week of comp-time she was getting for the overseas assignment and flew out to see her.

CHAPTER 7:
JUNE 2020 – PRISON

Aliceville, Alabama, was a cross-roads town of 2,500 in Pickens County near the Mississippi border. The roads crossing were route 17 to Selma, 100 miles south-east, and route 14 to Meridian, Mississippi, 75 miles south-west. Black took the afternoon flight from National to Birmingham, a couple of hours east of Aliceville, and rented a car to drive over. She'd read up on the town and found out that being near to those civil rights hotspots hadn't made much difference in Aliceville.

In the 1970s two local women, Maggie Bozeman and Julia Wilder, were convicted by an all-white jury for helping illiterate residents fill out absentee ballots. They went to prison, bringing on a protest caravan led by civil rights icon the Reverend Joseph Lowery, from Montgomery to the Pickens County seat. When their appeal finally made it to the federal level, a judge immediately threw out the entire case. As late as 1982, Bozeman testified before a congressional hearing on the Voting Rights Act, some voting in the county was done at an open table rather than in a booth, so that the choice could be seen. She said that police intimidated African-Americans by photographing people assisting them.

Aliceville's biggest industry was the 1,400-bed Federal Correctional Institution four miles northeast of town, which opened in 2013 as one of America's few federal all-female prisons. The town supplied most of the FCI's 350 guards along with the motel beds and meals that family visitors needed. Nearly all of those visitors were black or Hispanic, but there was no need for the Green Book now: the town had gone from majority-white under segregation to 75 percent black. Ironically, Aliceville's last economic boom had also come from a prison. In World War II the Army built a Prisoner of War camp there for 6,000 Germans from Rommel's Afrika Korps.

Black stayed overnight in the priciest place Expedia could find her: $60 for the Voyager Inn. That made her laugh: the hotel she'd stayed in on her last big case, in San Francisco, was the $400 Fairmont. The bargain motels out on the highway to the prisons read $30, with a weekly rate of $120. To her relief, at least she could get a beer with her aluminum plate of tacos at Los Dos Amigos. Pickens County as a whole was still dry, but Aliceville had voted to go wet in 2012.

FCI Aliceville was classified as a "medium-security" prison, with dormitory-style beds and generally free movement. However, it was also the destination for women whose crimes had been the most violent, and it had a rare SHU— a Special Housing Unit made up of single cells for protection and discipline. Only the most actively dangerous women were excluded from Aliceville and held in a tiny lock-down unit in the all-women's medical center on an old Air Force base in Fort Worth, Texas.

After passing through a series of chain-link fences topped with barbed wire and handing over her Glock, Black was met at the metal detector by the warden, Bobby LaGraux. His cowboy boots, crisp jeans, and gleaming white dress shirt confirmed him as the black Cajun she'd figured he was from their phone call, when he addressed her as "Chère" and ended with "OK, I'll see you, me." LaGraux had initially been wary about an FBI agent coming on a personal mission, but after hearing her tale had been only cooperative.

LaGraux apologized for asking her to go with a female guard into a room with a full-body scanner: "Since you're not here on official business, the regulations demand it. Jonesy, if anything indicates a search, come out and talk to me first. That's the best I can do. If it makes you feel any better, we all go through this every day too. Prison employees have always been a much bigger contraband problem than prison visitors. I'll wait out here. That's a system-wide regulation since the 2003 prison rape act— no men in a female screening area."

Black was soon glad the warden had asked Jones to call him before a search. The scanner had revealed what an x-ray machine would not: her tampon. That usually triggered an automatic "intrusive" search since, she was informed, it was a favored method for bringing in contraband. The warden waived the search, asked the guard to make a note of that on her I-pad, and instead asked Black to go into the bathroom and replace the tampon with one of the pads that were stocked there.

Again, he was apologetic: "Agent McGurk, I hate to do it. I sure wish you'd found some official reason for the visit." The warden then bent over backwards to make it up to her. He personally led her to La Shonda's unit rather than the visitors' hall, and told her they could wander anywhere they wanted as they talked.

"I heard you was looking for me, Ms. FBI," La Shonda said after they hugged. "But what I don't know is why." She looked pretty good to Black, no prison clothes, hair done nice, still trim and fly.

"That's because it's better if nobody but us knows, lady. The Clay Kings ain't gonna be no kind'a happy if they find out I was here, so let's keep it that way. You heard they took out Du'Shaunn, my baby cousin? No? Well, I think they did, and when I ran your name and saw you handled their accounts, I came straight away. I think I can keep you out of this. You know I'll really try to keep it 100 percent our little thing, but one way or the other, I need your help. I need the shot-callers."

"Damn, girl," mused La Shonda. "This is bad, bad timing. Since A. M. got out'a here in '18, I been working on early release from my 25, either my own pardon, or out on a bracelet through First Step. I put my time in: math teacher for the GED classes, counselor for suicide watch, I lead Bible study, I'm just an all-round good girl. It's about crunch time on the warden certifying my low RR, recidivism risk, and I don't need no complications right up in here right about now, getting him and the board thinkin' 'bout me and some old hoodlums."

"Well, sweet pea, then I'm a walking nightmare of a complication, because I need the 411 on the Kings' shot-callers, and I'd say you owe me. And if you don't owe me, I'd say you don't want no Ms. FBI skunkin' around your little plan. But hey, I'm interested, and I'll help if I can. Back up so I get the drift. A. M.? First Step? Talk to me."

"A. M. was my girl here, grandma really, since I came down from Danbury six years ago. Anne-Marie Johnson, Memphis crack banker for the Calis, and just like me, a walking, talking 'Niv-do' in the flesh. That's 'non-violent first-time drug offender,' the latest thing in prison reform. We the victims of racist mass incarceration, school-to-prison pipeline, new Jim Crow, ya know.

"First Step is the new law for federal Niv-do's, a bunch of other Nivs and even some Violents. It boosts our good credit days so we get on to electronic bracelets or half-way houses in a hurry. My lawyer says I can turn my last fifteen into three if I get certified for it, and then get a good RR."

"Oh, girl, you slick as always," laughed Black. "Jim Crow my ass— you used to call the math teacher racist for suspending your ass. We all laughed at that, since the whole class was brothers and sisters and they weren't suspended— just the one who told him to 'get the *** out my face!' But why you not certified if you so Niv-do?"

"Ah, that's the deal. You get First Step only if you didn't come in under sections on murder, assault, guns, drive-bys, sex crimes, and some other stuff, including the one hanging me up: causing injury during trafficking. They put lots of shootings and overdose claims in my indictment, basically anything the Clay Kings did and a lot of things I know they didn't, but I was pled to Niv-do's only. Anyway, if I win on that and the warden gives me the lowest RR, I'm home in three. And that's 12 early, you feel me?"

"Well, I'm not gonna get in your way," said Black. "Long as you give me what I need. But I gotta tell you, we FBI types know all about your grandma Anne-Marie and this prison reform crap. You can thank a prosecutor in Jersey for all that. Some guy put Jared Kushner's father away for white-collar stuff, and when he got to the White House with Trump he started pushing shorter sentencing."

"I don't know nothing 'bout no Kush-ner," whined La Shonda. "Everybody know it was Kim Kardashian got A. M. out, and that got the President on to Niv-do's and First Step."

"Oh yeah? Who do you think walked her into the oval office to see the president? Who do you think got a guy who wanted the Central Park Five executed to sign all this reform nonsense? And by the way, those rascals was guilty as sin on the assaults. Right from the start the cops said somebody else had raped the girl. They didn't need no bullshit 'I won't talk to the cops' confession from a low-life to know that."

"And as for this 'Niv-do' nonsense, I tell you, little one, folks at the Bureau just about had a heart attack from the video of Trump inviting Johnson to the State of the Union and getting her a standing ovation from Congress. There's nothing 'non-violent' about what she did, moving weight and Benjamins for Cali, or what you did for the Kings, or what you and I did back in the day, for that matter. Get real. Drug deals are enforced with violence, up and down the chain, and the whole thing's like dropping a bomb on a neighborhood. There was bodies everywhere in that Memphis operation that sweet little granny ran.

"This all reminds me of the same crap I kept hearing from a gang of old white terrorists I was chasing lately for stuff they did before yours and my mommas was even born. Called themselves the Weathermen, like they thought they could give us the news we needed. Bombed places backing our wars, but got off by claiming non-violence, because they called in warnings and nobody got killed. And that was some ripe bullshit— set off a bomb, you're saying someone can die if they're unlucky enough to come by. 'Course they actually tried to kill some cops and soldiers anyway, and were just too stupid to get it done. But that's another story..."

Now it was La Shonda who laughed. "Damn, Black, speakin' of Kimmy K, you a regular Kanye West, ain't you? All tough on the tribe. Next thing you know you be pulling a Bill Cosby, that sex fiend, tellin' HD boys to pull they pants up, like Coach Legion did. You remember that, him yellin' down the hall, 'I'm a Vagina-man. Don't want to see no young man's drawers!' All I's sayin' is, I'm not goin' back to the life, so what they wanna keep me here for?"

"Girl, you as dumb as those white Weathermen. They even got a new generation sayin' this stuff: Chesa Boudin, the son of two of the worst, who got three lawmen murdered in a robbery. He ran for DA in San Francisco, and won by promising to arrest ICE agents. Claims his dad ain't a danger to society anymore so they can let him out. Then again, he also thinks his parents' felony murder convictions were bogus because they 'just drove the getaway car.' Yeah, they did, like their gang had done before in another killing, and that's felony murder— especially when they lied to the cops, told them to put away their guns, and then their pals jumped out of the back of the truck and wasted 'em, oh yeah!

"Look, prison ain't just about keepin' you off the streets 'til you 'boost your RR' and are done with the life— although it did a good job of that with your so-called mass incarceration. Crime rates tripled from the '60s to the '90s, and putting all those folks in prison broke the trend, busted it way down today to where it first was. But prison is to punish too, remember. 'Do the crime, do the time' is there for a reason."

The two women looked at each other, and broke out laughing at the incongruity of where their lives had taken them. "OK, Black, go on. Now you Sandy Bullock, not the Blind Side one where she take the little brother to college, but the FBI one, just saw it the other night, where Mr. Star Trek ax her on stage what society need and she say, 'That would be harsher punishment for parole violators, Stan.' No applause so she add 'and world peace' and they go crazy.

"But let's get down to what you need. Just protect me, that's all. If anybody ever asks, you come here to advise me on my recidivism rating. I don't know nobody here connected to the Kings, or the DC game, for that matter. That's why I transferred. But if it leaks out up there, they be finding me down here, fo-sho."

Black left the prison an hour later, after a decent lunch— complete with vegan and Muslim options— with La Shonda and ten of her girls. They were a relaxed mix of black, white, and Hispanic, ages 20 to 60, whose crimes ranged from bank fraud to murder. True to the ethos of the incarcerated, though, nobody asked or mentioned their charges or acknowledged guilt, only their months served and their days to go on good behavior.

That's why all this rehabilitation is bullshit, Black thought as she noted the ladies' constant subtext of the unfairness of their situation. From the moment of arrest to the moment of parole, it was all about them, not their victims. Admitting guilt was a bad idea because it could only add time to your term. But admitting guilt was the actual "first step" toward the real rehabilitation of making it right with the people or communities you'd hurt.

A few of the older women had been transferred down to Aliceville from Danbury, Connecticut, with La Shonda in 2014. Danbury was the only federal prison for women in the Northeast, and the Bureau of Prisons decided to ship all its 1,200 inmates to the new Aliceville FCI, saying it needed the space for men. A group of senators from the region blocked that plan, arguing that the transfer would make it harder for children to visit their mothers: "These women clearly did something wrong in order to get to federal prison, but their kids didn't." BOP backed off and agreed to transfer just the 400 women who didn't live in the Northeast. La Shonda had volunteered to go with them, to get away from any connections with her old life.

The women laughed their way through lunch, energized by the novelty of having a visitor. La Shonda even had Black laughing with a story about gaming the system. Her lawyer had found a section in the First Step bill on dyslexia that a senator had added, on the theory that women ended up in the school-to-prison pipeline because they had a hard time reading. First she signed La Shonda up for the bill's screening and had her fail the reading test on purpose. Then La Shonda wrote the senator, whose daughter's difficulty in learning to read had spurred his interest, and thanked him for helping her find out why she had had such a frustrating time in school. Her letter and his supportive one in return were added to the "handicaps" portion of her request for early release under First Step. "Next thing you know," she told her hooting luncheon ladies, 50 girls take the screening and fail too…an epidemic of dyslexia, right here in Aliceville!"

La Shonda had given Black the five Clay Kings shot-callers from before her imprisonment in 2010. She couldn't say where they were today, or if they were even alive. She'd never been more than a contractor for the Kings, someone without a patron, which ironically had made her even more trusted as the money-counter. Once she'd transferred to Aliceville she'd completely lost contact, and that was just fine with her. Back in DC, Black gave the five names to Cass and Tono, who went off to check with CIU. Shirley called her back that night.

"OK, now we've got something. Four of them are no good— two in prison, one shot to death at a cousin's funeral, one gone straight, actually runs the Interrupters, the peace-makers that Youth Services pay to walk the streets, and we're not allowed to pump them. But this James Harris, there was no file on him, no snitches knew the name, so Gangs showed us their go-to method: they have all the middle and high school yearbooks since 2000. We pulled the ones east of the river, and found him as an eighth-grader at Ron Brown in 2005.

"He never even started HD, just disappeared into the muck— no social security, no driver's license, no record at all. When we showed the yearbook picture to Gangs, CIU, they lit up. They never knew his name, they just always call him the mysterious OGJ— original gangster J. That's what he's always gone by in the Kings, just "J," so none of the young snitches knew his real name. And he is indeed the grand old man, the top dog, a 30-year-old running the teens."

Black asked, "So, what's our next move?"

"Well, your next move is to sit tight. Our next move is to watch him 'til we catch him with a gun. The lieutenant says we can't go for a warrant on ten-year-old information from a CI, but if we get a suspicious act that corroborates him as a shot-caller, we can. Sorry, but it's still sit and wait for someone to screw up. But look, if he's still a shot-caller, it won't be long, because he probably handles the renting."

Sure enough, within a week of watching, Cass and Tono followed Harris to a beautifully-maintained coffee-colored '68 Cadillac he kept under a tarp in a driveway near his house on Dix Street, right below Clay Terrace. They ran the plates and got a name that matched a driver's license with Harris' picture but another name. That didn't surprise them; there'd been reports of Motor Vehicles employees selling fake licenses. What did surprise them was that right off the bat Harris stopped at an alley-house in South-East and came out with what was obviously, right down to its camo hide and carry straps, a tactical shotgun bag. "My God, what an idiot! That's why our job is so easy," chuckled Cass. They called the lieutenant, but she decided to hold off on the arrest and wait to see what good came out of the day.

It turned out to be the right call. The detectives followed Harris carefully down Route 301 through southern Maryland and across the bridge to Bowling Green, Virginia. When he turned into a nicely maintained ranch house in the white part of town, Tono shrieked "Bingo! We've got us a renter." When he came out without the bag, they just let him go, and drove off to the closest State Trooper barracks their dispatcher could find. The captain-on-duty there walked them through their story, confirmed with his staff that there had never been a report on that location, and cooked up a plan with them to take the renter down without disrupting the DC homicide investigation.

The plan hinged on Harris using the renter again. Cass and Tono would get a warrant to hide a GPS tracker on the Cadillac, based on the suspicious behavior that confirmed their CI's story. Then Virginia and DC would get warrants for SWAT no-knocks at the Bowling Green house and Harris' house, or wherever in DC the Cadillac went after picking up a gun. The two raids would be simultaneous so that neither low-life could warn the other.

CHAPTER 8:
JUNE-AUGUST 2020 — CAMPAIGNS

"OK, we've been waiting in the on-deck circle, letting the dust settle on the FedEx follies. But now it's finally our turn to bat." It was mid-June, and Cal Jones was addressing a full conference room. There were 25 supremely well-dressed people sitting around the table in Boeing's DC office in Vienna, Virginia. Clothes may not make the man and woman, but this bespoke crowd knew that they make a statement about income and importance.

The general stood at the head of the table. Fifteen Boeing staff and the heads of public relations firms filled the left side. The Mobe-Corp manager Charlene Wong and Kevin Smithson, the long-time international director of the Aerospace Industries Association, sat at the other end. But that's where the name cards stopped, in deference to the right side of the table. The fawning implication was that everybody should know them.

Starting at the far end, there were the Washington directors of the AFL-CIO and two of its largest non-governmental members, the International Association of Machinists and Aerospace Workers and the International Brotherhood of Electrical Workers. Then came the Washington directors of two unions that left the AFL-CIO in 2005 but still often allied with them, the Teamsters and the Service Employees International Union. Total membership represented at the table was 15 million.

And in the place of honor, right up next to Jones, sat Boeing's coup for this African sale: the head of the NAACP and the two most recognizable faces in American civil rights, Andy Young and Jesse Jackson. Nobody at the table doubted that of all the consulting fees Boeing had recently lavished on this project, the largest share had been directed to these two icons, 88 and 78 years old but radiating power and health in their sartorial majesty.

"Boeing's given me full authority, a blank check, and just one instruction: win. Failure is not an option here. When I met with leadership it was clear that this is about a lot more than one country and some gunships. It's the slippery slope they fear. If the Left can stop one sale over host country corruption, then they have a new tool to stop any sale, both in Africa and the Middle East.

"Now we know it's a small sale, about a billion dollars, something that wouldn't usually justify a campaign like this. But it's actually a big deal to Boeing, because the AC-130 conversions are done at Renton, in the Seattle suburbs, the plant with the 737-Max line. Work at that plant was about to be suspended in 2019 while the FAA was still deliberating on those two crashes, but then Trump's personal appeal to the CEO and a promise to explore more AC-130 deals kept the line hot.

"Just like with his ask from Lockheed Martin CEO Marillyn Hewson last year, he's thinking re-election. She kept a Lockheed plant open in Pennsylvania, and he must think that helps him hold it, by pointing to this specific factory that the great deal-maker kept on line. Lockheed had just won the huge presidential helicopter deal, and she owed him. And now she has a big chit in the future favor bank."

"Wait," interrupted Jesse Jackson. "I've run in both Pennsylvania and Washington state. I agree Trump's making sense in Pennsylvania, although no Democrat will win it anyway by promising to end its fracking boom, but no way he wins Washington, even with 20 factory deals. There must be something else going on with Boeing."

"Sir, that's what we thought too," replied the general, "until we checked with the Trump committee. Turns out Washington has been on their list from Day One. Trump lost to Hillary there by 16 points, but the third party, Johnson, got five. So they figure they'd get most of that, making it an 11 point split, for a swing of five and a half. Trump got a five point swing in Michigan last time, compared to Obama and Romney in 2012, and Washington's climate catastrophe governor just lost his referendum to tax fossil fuels— you know, the ones that power Boeing's plants and Boeing's planes?

"So they think Washington could be this year's Michigan, a shocker where Trump energizes his people more than the Dems energize theirs. And there have been stranger swings, like Gore dropping 22 points from Clinton in West Virginia in 2000— that 11-point swing on coal and guns cost him the election.

"So now that you know *why* we have to do this, let me ask our man on the Hill, Kevin Smithson of the AIA, to tell us *how*. Kevin ran the big Saudi sales campaign, U.S. Jobs Now, back in 1992, rolling everybody— not just Congress, but the Air Force, State Department, even the President. I still remember the tag line: *40,000 jobs, for us or the French.* Now we just want him to do it again. So settle in— we're not leaving today until all of us are comfortable with the plan and our assignments."

Smithson was a short white man in his mid-70s, with a full head of hair and a youthful and unassuming demeanor. He was not a climber: he had survived in his corporate world by decidedly not trying to stand out or supplant his superiors. His striped gray suit was indeed bespoke, but carefully understated, and his tie was soft blue, not power-red.

"OK, for the benefit of some of our distinguished allies who don't know our industry so well, I'm Kevin Smithson and I run foreign sales for the Aerospace Industries Association. Our CEO is former Senator and Secretary of the Army Ralph Halifax. We have a nice division of labor: he goes to the meetings in Vienna, Austria, and I go to the ones in Vienna, Virginia." Everybody laughed at this self-deprecation, which smoothly put the big shots on a higher plane.

"We're a trade association, sort of like the National Football League in that we're structured to be exempt from anti-trust laws. That means once one of our corporations signs an export deal, the competition is over. All our members then kick in to help the winner get government approval. Sort of all for one, once that one is picked.

"A bit on the approval process. I first got this job because I was a staffer for the Democrats on Senate Foreign Relations when they were just starting to use the laws on arms sales that were passed in that brief, post-Watergate surge on foreign policy that gave us the War Powers Act. Before that, it was just Shahs and Emirs leafing through glossy brochures at bedtime and circling the stuff they wanted. No congressional role at all.

"For decades our Achilles' heel has been human rights. A 1970s law, passed by a left-right alliance of isolationists, bars arms and training for 'gross and consistent' abusers of human rights— although it never defines just what that means. But Democrats especially get squishy when CNN shows some sultan's troops shooting protestors with American weapons— well, maybe not Democrats whose districts make the weapons." Smithson stopped, expecting a laugh, but everybody waited to see what the two most prominent Democrats in the room would do. Only when Young chuckled to Jackson, "Damn, ain't that the truth," did the rest explode in relieved laughter.

Smithson went on: "But as an industry we've gotten a lot better at dealing with human rights. For years I've been telling Congress and the press that we should use a weapons-based, not country-based approach. It's the little stuff, the hand-held gun, that kills people, not our big weapons, like fighters, AWACS, and refueling tankers. A buildup of major systems is almost always a deterrent to cross-border conflict. And internally, simply as a practical matter, you don't use F-15s against a crowd of demonstrators.

"The lefty groups ran a campaign back in the '90s equating us to the NRA, called 'AIA equals NRA, Pushing Weapons at Home and Abroad.' I could laugh them off in radio debates, saying I slept just fine at night, knowing that that our aircraft exports maintained peace in places where war had been common. But with the Yemen bombings, I can't say that anymore. And I sincerely hope it's the bizarre exception that proves the rule.

"Now, for years Congress kept adding informal 'holds' to the formal waiting period for a sale. So when Trump decided to go ahead with a big new package for Saudi despite the Khashoggi killing and the Yemen bombings, he short-circuited the process by citing emergency powers in the arms sales laws. That brought things to a head, with even the Republican Senate voting to block the deal, but he sustained his veto and we haven't heard 'boo' on human rights since. That was a watershed.

"We did have a little scare once on another front, democracy, on a bill in the'90s that banned arms sales to dictators. Strangely, the granddaddy of human rights groups, Amnesty International, didn't back it. They sort of adopted my argument, and only wanted to oppose weapons, not governments, with a history of abuse. But the rest of the lefties pushed this 'Code of Conduct' to floor votes in both Houses. We had a scare when it almost passed a House committee, which would have given it a privileged position inside a bigger bill and forced us to try to strip it out. But we had some allies who voted against the amendment in committee when we needed them and then voted for it on the floor when we didn't. Most members accepted the reality: hey, if we don't sell to dictators, who are we gonna sell to?"

Smithson paused for another laugh, then turned to the business at hand.

"Corruption is a new angle, one that brings in a whole new bunch against us, the Common Cause, good government crowd. It's very dangerous for us, and we have to win this out of the gate, put it to sleep. You see, both sides in Congress and virtually all the media from the Wall Street Journal to Amy Goodman love Transparency International, which rates government corruption around the world, and this new outfit that gave us the FedEx Files, World Financial Transparency. Now, we know WFT is all lefties— you can tell by who they've hired to run it, an old human rights hand. But that's just not the narrative around here. We're not going to win by attacking them. So, what do we do?

"The bill they've cooked up is a smart 'bridge' vote— a sneaky measure that doesn't ask people to come all the way over to opposing arms sales to Africa and the Middle East but puts them on the bridge that leads there. It freezes the arms deal until the president certifies that all cases of corruption or larceny identified by the FBI have been 'credibly' investigated and 'properly' prosecuted under American or Nigerien law, whatever that means. No mention of human rights or terrorism, so neither the right nor the left of the House will be driven away, and the small center loves this stuff. Nancy Pelosi has already promised a floor vote in October if it passes the Foreign Affairs Committee. Like I said, this is a smart campaign.

"Now, they're not perfect, and I think they've made one mistake, by giving in to this explosion of campus activism against the AID scholarships demanded by one of the president's wives that were routed to the children of the Nigerien elite. The bill freezes those too, and that's gold for us— we can sell the arms deal as an aid package not just for the terrorized but for education. I was hoping they'd go after the other wife's AFRICOM clinics too, but they must have figured out that would bleed off some votes.

Andrew Young spoke up. "It's been a long time since I was in Congress, trying to block arms to Portugal for their African wars. So educate me— why worry about the Democratic House if the Republican Senate won't pass it? Then there's no bill!"

Smithson replied, "Well, ambassador, as probably the only one here who was working in Congress when you were a Member, I can tell you things have changed a lot. Individual bills are rare now for important issues. Congress is so divided that they mostly legislate on appropriations bills, especially the Continuing Resolution when there's no agreement on the 13 subcommittee bills. Late in the year they put a 'clean' bill on the floor that just continues the existing limitations and funding levels for all government programs, and then all sides vote for it as the best possible deal.

"But that CR is never completely clean. Lots gets changed on the margins, in the dead of night during the House and Senate bargaining conference after each has passed their version of the CR. A member of the conference who really cares can make a case to leadership to include at least some of the restrictions that have passed one house. It would really be up to Pelosi, and that's why this bill scares us: the lefty groups driving this have shown some brains by carefully picking moderates as the lead sponsors, including one of Pelosi's closest allies. They won't let those crazy lefty ladies Pelosi hates anywhere near it. If we lose a House vote in October, we might well get stuck with something in conference on the CR. And whatever deal they make on a CR is gonna get past the 60-vote barrier that has become commonplace in the Senate."

"Gotcha," said Young. "Thanks for clearing up my old ideas. So, what's our plan to blow up the bridge?"

"Well, as General Jones said, when in doubt we've always gone back to basics— ignore our weakness, in this case the ins and outs of the corruption cases, and change the debate to one on our strength. And that is J O B S. Now, we all know that Niger won't really be sending any job-creating money America's way, since the loans will all be forgiven and become part of the federal debt. And anyone who took economics in college knows that by 'additionality' we'd get a lot of jobs in other sectors out of any real buy by Niger, whether its aircraft from France or from us, or even powdered milk from Australia.

"But I don't see WFT and Human Rights Watch having the chops to get into that. The arms control groups in the coalition don't even understand offsets— they keep saying that they cut the earnings of the exporters and should be subtracted from the claimed benefit of the deal to the American economy. But every offset has to go into the deal, so it's, well, offset by additional payments from the buyer. No, it'll all be about the corruption case, which we'll simply ignore as we focus on jobs.

"But jobs is by no means all we have this time. Through polling and focus groups we've worked up an additional angle, one that works almost as well with Democrats as Republicans, especially with the strongest Democratic group, African-Americans. It's all about R E S P E C T for minorities. And that's why we've reached out to you, Ambassador Young, and the Reverend Jackson, as our civil rights leaders.

"We first got the idea from the way Hillary Clinton disarmed lefty critics of Obama's Afghan war, by saying we had a moral duty to protect Afghan girls from being driven out of schools by the Taliban. Of course we didn't go to war to do that, and our Afghan pals won't do much better for women once we leave, but it was very powerful stuff. Our idea takes that approach, but sort of plays it off Black Lives Matter. We polled a lot of push phrases, but the highest response came from: Don't Africans deserve freedom from terrorism too? Off the charts, not just with African-Americans, but with whites and Hispanics as well."

With that, Smithson began to run through a PowerPoint proposal for a reprise of the legendary 1963 civil rights "March on Washington for Jobs and Freedom" that Young and Jackson had attended. This one would have the same name and rally at the same spot on the same day— the Lincoln Memorial on August 28. It would start with a $5 million media buy, using all the main papers and networks, featuring images and videos of actors.

Some actors would play wholesome American workers saying they were proud to make equipment that would help free Africans from terrorist thugs, interspersed with stock footage of U.S. Army medics treating patients in an AFRICOM clinic. Others would play troubled African villagers and grateful Boeing-Clyburn students in their American college shirts and ball caps saying "thanks." Special buys in regional papers, TV stations, and targeted web ads would feature the "students," all in the local college colors.

The buy was the classic Washington way to generate interviews and news stories, and create an environment in which outlets wanted op-eds by the civil rights and union leaders. The business side of the paper or station didn't need to tell reporters and editors to cover the issue raised in the ads. They could see and hear the ads and calculate the size of the buy themselves. And so the buzz begins.

The brazen use of the original March on Washington would generate critical opinion pieces and maybe even leftist demonstrations, Smithson acknowledged, but he argued that it would be all to the better. A Black Lives Matter or Code Pink disruption, let alone an "anti-fa" attack, would force congressional opponents of the sale to pull in their claws. Each critique or action would lead to requests for a response from Young and Jackson, giving them yet another chance to ask whether Africans should have to live with terrorism. "Please, God, let AOC and Omar try to argue with Andrew Young and Jesse Jackson," Smithson said. The room cracked up again, not even waiting for the approval of the icons now. The deal was sealed.

"That's a loser every time. You can say: 'We fought apartheid in South Africa so Africans could be free of state terror; now we're fighting for Africans to be free of religious terror.' Tucker Carlson and Fox and Friends will eat it up, a chance to zing the Black Lives types. And Fox, that's the way to reach our true audience of one. If Donald Trump decides he really wants this, he'll roll anybody in Congress we can't bring over ourselves.

"But we don't want it to get to that. We want the same outcome we had in 1992, when Bill Clinton came out for the Saudi sale before Bush did. We'll know we're good when the Democratic candidate calls on Trump to add an economic aid package to the arms deal. Just to encourage that we've signed Dale Earnhardt Jr. to do a bunch of ads and appearances in the 2016 flip states— Pennsylvania, Ohio, Michigan, Wisconsin. He's retired, just running a team now, but his name recognition and favorables are still in the 90s with all the male racial demographics. If anything can get the Democrat on board, it'll be Junior's ads.

"By the way, Earnhardt has some stones. He loves a fight. He reminded me that the coal companies once hired him to take on the global warming crowd with a bunch of 'clean coal— cheap electricity' ads. In 2013 his NASCAR team even ran an all-black Chevy with 'Clean Coal' written across it!"

Everybody laughed at that, except the former coal miner who ran DC for the AFL-CIO. "Hey, hey, easy on coal now, we're still here." he shouted, boisterously. "I autographed that car, Regan Smith's 7, right before Keselowski split off the front end— put him right into the wall; last turn, last lap at Daytona. I say we ask Junior to put out an African freedom car, or maybe just hang these fancy Boeing machine guns on his National Guard car, and drive Andy and Jesse to the Lincoln Memorial for their speeches. Boogity, Boogity, Boogity— let's go racin'!"

* * *

Even the generally apolitical Mar'Shae McGurk was aware of the Jobs and Freedom campaign by mid-August. Black didn't read the papers much and she barely knew who Jesse Jackson was, let alone Dale Earnhardt Jr., but she could hardly see a Metro bus go by or take the subway across town without seeing the wall to wall ads. It took her a while to make the connection to her case, though, because none of the ads actually mentioned Niger— they all had the tag line, "Congress— Support the Freedom from Terror aid package: 10,000 American workers and 500 million African women are counting on you."

Black's campaign was going pretty well, too. It took her team of financial specialists less than a week in Niamey to find the offset invoices in the Finance Ministry's files. They created background summaries on the private and government officials who had signed them, using translators brought in by a French language-training firm to avoid both State Department and Nigerien leaks. After work the translators would be driven straight back to their hotel and monitored so no Nigeriens could approach them for information.

Black provided the summaries to Nigerien police for investigation, but there appeared to be no follow-up. In America she could have squeezed these lower echelons to get up towards the top of the conspiracy, but in this case her boss decided that the best she could do was ask Treasury to issue U.S. visa and banking sanctions on the officials and their relatives. The State Department didn't object, so a few Boeing-Clyburns would be coming home.

And it was just as easy for the New York office to match the invoices to the amounts that disappeared in the over-pricing. Most of it seemed to come out of the offsets for Mobe-Corp's training and operations support rather than for Boeing's aircraft and armaments. There were certainly some adjustments in Boeing's invoices, but they cut both ways, indicating normal business practices. Apparently the well-paid Boeing executives had learned the hard way not to fish for small fry, and were studiously content to hold onto their big fish, procurement by the U.S. Government. Most of Boeing's annual profit margin came from military rather than commercial aviation. Mobe-Corp, though, had some hungry mouths at the lower levels, which led them to dine with the Nigeriens. But when Black's team added up all they'd eaten, it came to just a fraction of the $300 million missing in the Mobe-Corp offsets.

That's when the case got interesting. Most of the receipts from the over-invoicings went first to a single Delaware account whose beneficial owner's name had, of course, been withheld. Rather than engage in a lengthy legal fight that would have to break new ground, Black's team used its existing domestic authorities and foreign agreements to recreate the electronic movement of money from Delaware through a series of off-shore accounts. Unfortunately, the trail ended in Somaliland, Eritrea, and Yemen, countries where the FBI had no presence or leverage. At least $200 million disappeared there. One morning Black emailed her boss a draft request to the State Department to cooperate with the FBI Legal Attachés nearest those countries in arranging travel and setting up interviews at the banks. By noon she was called to a meeting in the Director's office.

The Director! An apprehensive Black couldn't figure that out. A Director rarely got down in the weeds of operations by questioning an agent, and she'd never heard of the current one, Christopher Wray, doing it. That would be considered almost an insult to the executive assistant directors, who were God-like enough for her. When she walked in the door, she saw the reason for Wray hosting the meeting: four of the six executive assistants were there— national security, criminal, intelligence, IT— meaning that whatever issue was on the table cut across all their jurisdictions, so none of them could be the host.

"Agent McGurk," said the Director, "I don't think I've seen you since the press conference for the Weather-cat indictment. I'm glad to see you seem to have survived the outcome, and are doing well in your new job. Hell, I'm glad to see that I survived that dog of a case! I should have known from Mark Felt's conviction that anyone here who touches the Weathermen regrets it…" Black nodded politely. In this setting, that was the smartest thing to do. She still had no idea what she was doing here, five levels over her head, sitting next to the executive assistant directors and listening to this chit-chat. She just knew it was not a good place to be.

"I know this is not your usual noon meeting. But we're here because I had an unusual 10 o'clock myself. I was called to the White House to sit with the head of the CIA, the Attorney General, the National Security Advisor, the Chairman of the Joint Chiefs of Staff, and the director of the Defense Intelligence Agency. Any idea why, Agent McGurk?"

This called for at least a comment, so Black made the safest one: "Absolutely no idea, sir."

"Because bad news travels fast. Your request to interview bankers in these three countries has set off alarm bells in the intelligence agencies. Which ones, you don't need to know. The point is that, as I feared from the beginning of this case, sooner or later we were going to bump up against not garden-variety criminal and corporate corruption that uses these essentially ungoverned countries as the new Switzerland, but our own government's operations.

"You'd think that the intelligence agencies would have enough money by now, after almost 20 years of congressional generosity since 9/11. But appropriated money comes with oversight, employment regulations, formal complaints, pensions...oh, and the paper trail and leaks that come from reporting to the Intelligence committees and the Defense Appropriations subcommittees. In any war, there's always something somebody wants to do, maybe even needs to do, that can't quite endure that kind of sunshine.

"Apparently our intelligence agencies used to just ask other countries to do the tasks they couldn't, and we'd return the favor another time as part of some congressionally-notified operation. The few congressional leaders who had to be in on that were fine with it, but it became effectively illegal late in the 1980s because of the special counsel's work in the Iran-Contra arms scandal. We'd gotten help in that deal from Israel, Saudi, even some Asian sultan, in Brunei, a country I'd never even heard of. So now, if Congress doesn't appropriate funds, or at least know about it, we who get our salaries from Congress can't use our time to arrange for someone else to do it.

"But McGurk, what if some private company somehow got it in their head, all on its own, to do something that an intelligence agency also wanted done? Let's suppose they siphoned money off an arms sale offset, put it in a working account overseas, and hired contractors for missions to disrupt terror cells. And let's suppose those contractors happened to chat with old pals in the intelligence agencies about where those cells were housed. Sounds far-fetched, completely illegal, right? Informally suggesting, winking, and nodding— how's that different from straight-out asking? Now nobody in this room is confirming or denying such practices, but I will point out to you that the same sort of legal fiction is what elects our leaders in the first place, these 'uncoordinated' campaigns that aren't subject to the legal funding limits.

"With that as background, the purpose of this meeting is to tell you that the FBI has been formally ordered by the National Security Advisor, in writing, with certification of legality by the White House Counsel and the Attorney General, to leave the accounts you found alone, for reasons of possible 'irreparable damage' to national security. That order stays in my safe, its existence is code-word classified, and you are never to mention it to your staff or anybody unless they have the right code-word. And that's the people you see sitting at the table with you right now. Your immediate supervisor is aware of the general situation, but you and he are not to discuss it or ever divulge it.

"For what it's worth, this is really no big loss to the outcome of the case. We'd have been beaten before trial anyway— it's called 'gray-mail,' when a defendant threatens to expose an operation so the government drops the case. And probably after trial too: hell, the guy, Elliott Abrams, who got the arms money from the Sultan of Brunei, was convicted, pardoned, and is back in government again at the top of the foreign policy chain. So now's as good a time as any to clear the deck. Make your case without the foreign banks. Got it?"

Black absorbed all this quietly. She decided not to answer that question, and just nodded her head politely. Just because Wray worked in a SCIF, a Sensitive Compartmented Information Facility, that blocked electronic and audio monitoring from the outside, didn't mean he wasn't taping this talk from the inside. She'd worked enough cases based on surveillance tapes to know that staying silent was the safest course.

Black didn't know it, but that same week she was becoming dangerously well-known in two other places. One was at Mobe-Corp. At the request of its employees who had received formal notice of FBI subpoenas for their bank accounts, and of its Nigerien partners who'd been tipped off by their co-conspirators inside the Finance Ministry, Mobe-Corp had worked its government contacts to find out about the FedEx task force and its leader.

The other place of unwelcome notoriety was at the apartment the Clay Kings' big dogs and shot-callers kept on the Terrace just for their meetings. They had a network too, and had heard from a source they paid in CIU that an old Simple City girl gone straight named Mar'Shae McGurk was going out with Cass and Tono on her cousin's murder, and she was trying to pin it on the Kings. That explained a lot of the surveillance they'd been feeling lately. It was starting to cut into sales, and that was never a good thing.

PART III:

THE CATCH

CHAPTER 9:
SEPTEMBER 2020 – ELECTIONS

"What just happened? We went into the recess with Mobe-Corp suspended, not just from this deal but from all government contracts. We come back and DOD and the CIA have issued public reports absolving both Boeing and Mobe-Corp for their few 'bad apples' and announcing the continuation of the Niger program. I mean, they had a nice rally, so what? What turned this around? We had 140 Members and 30 Senators on our letter, including half of Foreign Relations and Foreign Affairs! How did they get rolled?"

It was the day after Labor Day, and a very frustrated Mary Magdalen Carter, fresh from a glorious month of sailing, reading legal thrillers, and watching Amazon Prime on Martha's Vineyard, looked at the long faces around the conference table at WFT. Nearly all of the 40 activists— representing religious, peace, human rights, and "good government" groups— had been on their well-earned vacation in August, and were just hearing about the disaster that had unfolded in their absence.

"Well," said Human Rights Watch's Pierre Nkumbo, "the AIA wasn't taking a vacation. They did a letter too, with less Members but more impact. Take a look at the signatures on this letter to the Secretary of Defense and the Director of the CIA, sent in early August and kept private until Defense News got hold of it last week, when it was doing a story on the FedEx decision."

Nkumbo passed around copies of the letter, on which he had circled each name at the bottom and added his own notes. He began to read: "Chair, Defense Appropriations Subcommittee; Ranking Member, Armed Services Subcommittee on Readiness; Ranking Member, Intelligence Committee; Chair, Armed Services Subcommittee on Seapower and Projection Forces...Only 12 names, but they include the chair and the ranking Republican on the three committees DOD and the CIA care about in the annual bills, plus the chair and ranking member of three Armed Services Subcommittees.

"We have to read this the way the Secretary and Director did: as a terrifying display of strength by the AIA. This is AIPAC-level stuff, getting the big egos to share a letter in almost immediate response to a request about a complex and tough issue. That itself sends a message to other Members, that even hesitating makes you suspect. Now, we need to fight on and see if we can convince our side that it's still worth offering the freeze bill as an amendment.

"After all, even a losing roll call vote, a hard whip count, would help us in future fights. But my sense is that with the letter and the decision, this is over. Our Members will be able to smell a loser, and they hate to lose. So we probably need to cut down our ask pretty substantially. I think our donors will understand, and in fact will respond to, just how outgunned we are…no pun intended."

The head of the Quaker lobby, the Friends Committee on National Legislation, spoke up. "Well, I'm never one to shy away from a losing fight." Laughter interrupted him, since everybody knew the story of him leading a flotilla of rowboats in Norfolk harbor that briefly trapped an aircraft carrier bound for Iraq in 2005, the same ship that South Africa barred from a port visit later in its journey. "But I respect Pierre's judgment on these matters. He's been at it a lot longer than me. But here's one thought. We have Jim McGovern, the chair of the Rules Committee, on our letter. Weren't you celebrating that as our most powerful message— that he could hold up and complicate amendments DOD and the CIA want on the floor if they fight us? Can't we ask him to negotiate for us now?"

"It's true, I was pretty excited about that," replied Nkumbo, "especially because he'd been hoodwinked into backing military aid to the Ugandan dictator, during all that Kony 2012 hoopla. You remember, that bizarre Acholi rebel who wasn't even in Uganda? For a decade Museveni kept him floating around as a threat, both for domestic control and to grab as much aid as he could from AFRICOM. So yeah, it was good to have McGovern back in the human rights fold, and he sure learned at the master's feet how to use his Rules power.

"When Jim staffed the committee for Joe Moakley back in the '80s, Moakley threatened Dick Cheney with no floor amendments on the DOD bill if he wouldn't let an Army officer be interviewed by his Speaker's Task Force that was investigating the slaughter of the Jesuit professors in El Salvador. He got the officer, who'd actually heard the High Command talking about planning the murder and trying to blame it on the rebels. That helped Moakley and Jim end the war. But I think Jim will know pretty quickly that he won't be able to sustain any threat on this one— and a Rules chairman losing a Rule? That's not where you want to get a hard whip count!"

* * *

Black was strolling down the corridor towards her office after a morning of sitting with federal prosecutors, finalizing the list of evidence they could use in plea bargaining. There was a gaggle of her agents outside the office, obviously waiting for her. "OK, what's up? Aren't we about done with this case?"

Hardly, it turned out. One of the records teams had, as a matter of course, entered the names of the signers of the congressional letter to DOD and the CIA into the search engine of the Federal Election Commission. In each of the 12 cases there had been a sharp spike in contributions in the second quarter, from April to June. A little digging found that about 80 percent came from offices and employees at Mobe-Corp. A little more digging in databases for national and state party committees and "uncoordinated" campaigns allied with the signers showed the same spike.

"Huh. Nothing for Boeing?," Black asked.

"No, they were big and regular funders of everybody on these committees, so I don't think they needed to back up their request like Mobe-Corp did," said the head of the record team. "I mean, they fund everything, all the time, from high school marching bands to entire universities. They used to endow chairs just for aeronautics professors, but now there's even a Boeing professor of government at the University of Washington, just to make the point that they control the government, so they might as well fund the people who study it. Being called the Senator or Congresswoman from Boeing is no insult in Washington State. It's a valued compliment for both parties."

Black told the team to go off and do some more digging on the other typical pay-off, jobs for family members. Members and their top staff had to take a one-year "cooling off" period before being paid to "seek official action" from anybody in Congress. Unwritten understandings that they would be hired after a year at a salary far exceeding their congressional pay were often presaged by jobs for their spouses and children.

Sure enough, the lists published and constantly updated by a "good government" group, the Project on Government Oversight, known as POGO, had some hirings of the twelve's spouses and children in the past six months, at both Boeing and Mobe-Corp and at their top lobbying, law, and communications firms. Black's superiors didn't think the compensation was high enough to make a strong case, and told her to stick with the election contributions.

Investigating Congress was a delicate matter. Black could have stormed into the offices of the Mobe-Corp executives who'd made the election donations and offer immunity for sworn statements, but she was told to hold back, and first plan a sting on her real targets, the 12 Members of Congress. Her superiors would have to debate and approve each part of the plan because of the contentious history of FBI investigations of Congress.

The FBI had paid a steep price in congressional support after its 1979 "Abscam" operation, in which a fictional Arab sheik offered bribes in exchange for a personal immigration bill. The operation resulted in seven felony convictions of sitting Members, but both sides of the aisle united in protest of the FBI's tactics. Oversight hearings exposed tactics the FBI preferred to keep under wraps, and the usual pro-FBI orientation in congressional budgeting was threatened. A Lebanese-American senator founded the Arab-American Anti-Discrimination League, which bitterly criticized both the FBI's story line for the sting and the name Abscam, which sounded like it derived from "Arab." The FBI formally renamed the operation Abdul-scam, after the name of its fictional sheik, but tensions still ran high with the Hill.

The bureau had then been cautious in its congressional investigations for more than two decades, until a bribery complaint led to the taping of Congressman William Jefferson accepting cash from an FBI informant in a 2005 sting. Jefferson told the informant that he needed the cash to "motivate" Atiku Abubakar, the Nigerian vice president, to approve the informant's business deal. This was the same "Tiku" who was later accused by a Senate Committee of money-laundering to pay his pledge to American University. A raid of Jefferson's house then uncovered the cash in his freezer.

An unprecedented 2006 follow-up raid of Jefferson's office in Congress set off a firestorm of bipartisan protest. President Bush froze the FBI's review of the seized documents, and FBI director Robert Mueller threatened to resign if they were returned to Jefferson. An appeals court eventually ruled that some aspects of the raid were unconstitutional, because the FBI agents reviewed legislative documents in search of criminal ones. Jefferson was still convicted, largely on other evidence, and sent to prison.

Black had her team track down the few surviving agents from the Abscam leadership. Jan Bryant had been a key strategist, and he was eager to impart his lessons. Bryant was a bear of a man in his early '80s, living in a modest retirement community in Petersburg, Virginia. "Well, well, a black woman in a black pant suit," he said, when she introduced herself to him during his lifting routine in the community's gym. "I'm damn glad we never saw anything like that in our day!"

Black stood still, not quite believing her ears. "Ha, the pant suit, I mean! Got ya there! I think beautiful girls like you should be in skirts, and I'll go to my grave saying it. Too bad you're here on official business in today's politically-correct FBI. Otherwise I know you'd be throwing yourself all over this Hoochie Coochie Man. We didn't have many women agents in my day, but we called all the secretaries *** Buddies International, for good reason."

Black relaxed— he was certainly a wild man, maybe an incorrigible sexist, but not the white racist he'd been pretending. She decided to play along.

"Don't flatter yourself, oh so-Special Agent Bryant. Even when you might've been handsome, like 50 years ago, I would've passed. I'm a lesbian."

"Ah, you got me back. Playing for the wrong team; what a loss to mankind. But maybe I can still cure you like James Bond cured Pussy Galore... what, you never saw the movie Goldfinger, with his flying circus of dykes? Oh Lord, standards have clearly fallen. Hey, I'm just playing with you. I had you checked out. I know how good you were at Cold Case.

"For what it's worth, I think you got screwed when Justice traded that Weatherwoman, the one you could have built a murder case on, for some cock and bull story about the Weather-cat. The top tier of Justice were idiots when I was there and they're clearly idiots now. Probably comes from sucking up to Congress on a daily basis. Or maybe only ass-kissers and ass-coverers can rise to the top of any bureaucracy. But speaking of Congress..."

Bryant told Black it was time for his daily four-mile walk. Off he stormed, talking for the entire hour it took. Black huffed along next to him, holding her phone up to record him.

"Now, what we learned in Abscam is that only the stupidest Congressman, or one who's desperate to avoid a bankruptcy scandal, is ready to play from the get-go. You might get the rare one, like we did, the one who popped right up with, 'I've got larceny in my heart.' He was the one whose wife posed in Playboy."

Bryant started singing as he powered along, "Lovely Rita, meter maid, where would I be without you?" Seeing that Black didn't know that reference either, he got back to business. "Jesus. You have heard of the Beatles, haven't you? Anyway, that's not what you want, the loose cannon, the crazy one. You want to show that the typical Member doing the typical thing can go down for bribery. That's what changes behavior. Now, nobody will plead until the first one loses. You have to win a trial, and for that you need the videotaped moment where someone doesn't just say 'Yes' to a bribe, but actually asks for it.

"We got a bunch of those moments in Abscam, and the convictions made Members of Congress and scumbag Jersey politicians look over their shoulder for 25 years. But it wasn't easy. You need an airtight story for your sting that leads them, not you, to be the first to suggest the payoff. That's the key. Forget those assholes from Justice telling you that judges almost always rule for the prosecution and inform the jury that the conduct in the case doesn't rise to the legal definition of entrapment. Juries can nullify that in a heartbeat. Remember, the judge told the Mayor-for-Life's jury that the bitch may indeed have set him up, but it wasn't entrapment."

That was one reference Black knew, both from her grandmother and the constant guff she got from other agents when they found out she was from east of the river. But the late Marion Barry got the last laugh, living on in statue outside the district building and in legend, both for his crimes and his comeback from them, when the District's black voters joined him in telling whites to "get over it," and made him mayor all over again.

CHAPTER 10:
DECEMBER 2020 TO MARCH 2021 – THE STING

Black pushed back from the bar at Busboys, her neighborhood spot for millennials, one of the few clubs in DC where blacks, whites, and Asians mixed. The bartender zapped her phone for her coconut tofu bits. She alternated between her old life and her new each time she came to Busboys for dinner. Few homies from Benning Heights had ever heard of tofu, and few riders at her Soul Cycle on 14th Street would ever have the joy of licking the sauce from a rack of ribs from their fingers.

She wandered toward the sounds of laughter coming from the performance space at the back of the restaurant. A hand-lettered sign on the door read "IPS Holiday Party," reminding her that she had two weeks to get her Christmas shopping done. Pushing inside, Black saw a fiftyish white woman dressed up like a Daddy Warbucks cartoon— spats, black tails and a top hat— leading a half dozen people, ages 20 to 40 it seemed, one black, one Asian, the rest white, in a play. They had line cards to read, but the woman seemed to have it all memorized, and prompted them when they faltered.

The players had placards looped around their necks: Big Banker, Capitalist Media, Low-Wage Industrialist, Wall Street Leech, Prison-Industrial Complex, Best Congress Money Can Buy, and Fossil-Fueled Think Tank. The plot had something to do with a FedEx envelope containing the names of people to be fired just before Christmas, with the various players finding out that they too were on the list. At the end all the players chanted, "In the end— even capitalists— lose under capitalism," to much laughter and applause from about 20 mostly white people in their 50s and 60s.

As the director came out to get a drink, Black said, "Hey, loved the drama— but why FedEx? I didn't get that."

"Oh, that's a riff on the arms deal that got exposed, the one in Africa. You know about that?" The woman was energetic and friendly, focusing her eyes and interest firmly on Black alone. Black was surprised to feel a twinge of intense interest too for this bubbly white lady in costume.

"That's funny— I actually do a little work on that case. So what's IPS, and how did you get to be the artistic director?"

"Institute for Policy Studies, the movement think-tank. I'm Naomi. You must not come here a lot: it's where we do a lot of our talks. Andy, the owner, he's on our board."

"I'm Mar'Shae, and this is actually my regular dinner spot. But what movement? You'll have to explain that one."

"Well let me get my drink, and I will, gladly," said the woman. "What about you, can I grab you one too?"

"Had my one beer already— I'm a cheap date. But fizzy water with lemon would be good."

Just then two elementary school girls, one black, one white, came running up from inside the performance space. The black one gasped out, "Mommy, you promised, a coke, a coke, please! And one for Julie, too?"

"Ok, but Deb, you two wait here and say 'hi' to Mar'Shae. I'll be right back."

Black chatted with the funny little girls until Naomi brought the drinks. "Man, that's not cheap. Busboys is the land of the $20 Margarita, but I always try to get something when we have an event. Andy never charges for the space, so he deserves some of our cash."

Naomi and Mar'Shae sat and talked, long after the rest of the think-tank players had gone home. Once Naomi explained what the "movement" was and once Black explained exactly what "work" she did on the FedEx Files, they looked at each other and both broke into laughter. Without saying it, they knew they were laughing at the same awareness: they were political opposites who already knew they wanted to be romantic partners. It was the beginning of Black's first real relationship in years.

Whether it was Black Lives Matter, big business, "climate change," Trump, or Bernie Sanders, Naomi was a true lefty believer and Black was an unconvinced observer. Naomi's liberal arts college education and her job promoting progressive mantras contrasted with Black's graduate work in public policy statistics and her job of marshalling proof that would stand up to scrutiny in court. The both enjoyed the times that Black was certain enough about her facts to argue bitingly back, like when she cited studies showing that cops facing a gun actually shot black suspects significantly less often than white ones. She followed that with, "the only black life that's gonna matter if somebody draws down on me is gonna be mine!"

But their political differences were irrelevant compared to the common values they discovered. Both women naturally tolerated, even respected, and could be fiercely loyal to friends and family whose ideas and affiliations they opposed. They were proud of each other's devotion to their work, even though they disagreed on most of it. And they especially bonded over Deborah, whom Naomi had adopted as a newborn, shrugging off criticism of "colonial" adoption by the righteous black summer interns at IPS. Black called her deb-OR-ah, as a joke on black names, and took her to breakfast on Saturdays with Mary Olive's youngsters while Naomi slept in. It wasn't time yet for Naomi to bring the white girlfriend east of the river, but it was getting there.

* * *

The Monday after she met Naomi, Black submitted the plan she'd worked up with Bryant. Outside of her boss, only the top three officials in the bureau knew about it. Later that week, unbeknownst to her, Attorney General Barr had called House Speaker Nancy Pelosi personally to ask if he and FBI director Wray could come in for a "no staff, no notes" session with the Big Four, the House and Senate leaders, in the House SCIF. Pelosi, Minority Leader Kevin McCarthy, and their Senate counterparts Mitch McConnell and Chuck Schumer had been talking for a few minutes while waiting for them, trying to figure out what had brought on this rare request.

Contrary to the impression made by their constant public disparagement of each other's concepts and conduct, the leaders were respectful colleagues and worked well together once the doors were closed. They were really the only people on Capitol Hill who felt each other's pain of trying to leading a fractious caucus driven by fractious constituencies. Another thing they shared was the ability to keep the remarkable secrets that tended to pop out in these "no staff, no notes" sessions. It would likely expose them to the sort of "hard cases" that Justice Oliver Wendell Holmes said "make bad law" and so shouldn't be treated as precedents.

"I agree with Mitch, I much prefer 'no staff, no notes' for the first shock of a nasty issue. I remember when I was ranking on Intelligence, and the CIA people slipped in an elliptical reference to water-boarding while briefing Porter Goss and me. They try to take stunned silence as approval, because then they can say, "Hey, it's on the briefing paper, and you didn't object."

McCarthy laughed. The presidential election was over, and the lack of tension was a relief for all of them. "God, Nancy, let's not get back into all that. Anyway, didn't Obama, that great humanitarian, solve the torture and rendition problems by just drone-killing them all?"

"OK, OK, boys and girls, let's focus here," cut in Schumer. "Barr's bringing in the FBI, not the CIA. Maybe it's something about the president who keeps on giving, and his financial house of cards? Well, here they are."

Barr and Wray were led into the SCIF. The leaders rose and chatted with them, exchanging brief requests for favors in the grand DC tradition of not letting an opportunity to raise money or move issues pass by unused. Then they all sat at the conference table.

"Well, Bob, here we are," said the Speaker. The House and Senate counsels are outside, as you asked. What's up?"

"Thanks, Madame Speaker, and we brought our top constitutional lawyer too, just in case she can be helpful with them on some details after we talk. We're here because of Abscam, sorry, Abdul-scam, and William Jefferson."

"Oh Lord," said McConnell. "Not again. What have our rascals been up to now?"

"I'll have Chris handle that in a minute, but let me just say that I think in both those cases Justice should have had an informal meeting like this, and they paid a big price because they didn't. We want to brief you on a criminal investigation and the tactics we plan to use. It's that simple. No hidden agenda, no attempt to 'get you on board.' Now, as you can understand, we're not here for approval, we and I guess you too can't do that constitutionally, but we want to listen, today, or in a couple of days, to what you think, before we set it in motion."

Barr turned it over to Wray, who made a very general, very careful synopsis of the situation: an intense concentration of funding from new and interested donors to 12 members who put together a supportive letter to the administration on a procurement dispute. Then he got down to it.

"We'd like to tear this nexus apart, from the donors to the members, and see if we find a clearly corrupt payoff. But it's the judgment of our Public Corruption unit that we're too late, that the proof is buried in the past. They've instead proposed a sting on the 12, as they often do when we're dealing with suspect regulators, a city council or a mayor, and I can't turn that down just because these officials happen to be in Congress.

"Our intent is to steer clear of congressional privilege. This sting will never physically touch the Hill like in Abdul-scam and Jefferson. The 12 will be approached through their campaign committees. They'll be invited to a law office downtown to discuss possible campaign donations, and be offered a clear trade. I can see no need now for any subpoenas involving their homes or offices. If for some reason such a need develops, we'll tell you in advance."

Pelosi immediately homed in on the hidden subtext. "Come on, Mr. Wray, any computer run could turn up dozens of correlations of contributions and actions, nearly all, I'm sure, wholly due to common interests and district concerns. What makes this case so special that you are planning to risk a breach with Congress to go after a correlation? What are we missing here?" That was her diplomatic way of asking, "what aren't you telling us?"

Barr jumped in. "All right, what I can tell you is that this case developed from a high-profile one we were already actively investigating, the FedEx Files. As just you four and the Intelligence eight know, the President already had to intervene once in this case to protect a national security operation. He signed that order limiting the FBI on a very specific issue of foreign wire transfers by banks used by our anti-terrorist operatives. But there's no national security argument against catching payoffs to Members of Congress. If we don't treat this like any other public corruption case, we too are open to, shall we say, misinterpretation of our motives."

Black soon had her approval, along with immediate overtime help from every office she approached. Within two weeks she had created a fully-registered lobbying firm, complete with six agents playing lawyers, the requisite office staff of secretaries and assistants, and a tony K Street office. The bureau's thinking was that lawyers would make their targets more comfortable in skirting legal boundaries than purely political lobbyists. To account for their recent arrival on the scene, the agents, all of whom actually had law degrees, pretended to be successful lobbyists of state legislatures who had met for years at conferences and finally decided to go federal together. By design, none of the claimed states were home to the 12 targets. As Barr and Wray had promised, they hedged against the expected congressional anger in the aftermath of the case by holding all their meetings with Members and staff off the grounds of Congress and its office buildings.

A retired agent who had become a lobbyist for military contractors helped Black script the initial contacts so they would feel authentic. As with the CIA, nobody ever really retired from the FBI club. Part of the drill was to be on call to help when asked. Nobody mentioned pay, nobody filed any paperwork, but this tradition effectively multiplied available expertise many times over.

First the secretaries called the campaign committees of the twelve to set up phone appointments with the campaign manager or finance director. The lobbyist then would explain that the firm had a client in the defense industry who wanted to "provide substantial backing" to the Member, and set up a meeting at the K street office. That was business as usual, and Black's people had no trouble getting the meetings. The Senators insisted that this first meeting be taken by the campaign manager or the finance director, but the House members, with smaller budgets, were happy to take the first meeting themselves, usually bringing one of the campaign staff to handle the details of the contributions.

Financial reports from the fall election were ready to file, and it was time to start the train rolling again. The average Senate race costs about $10 million, and the average House race about $2 million. But a competitive race, or even a serious primary challenge, could cost a lot more. Every

Member also had to kick in for the party's efforts, and Members on the rise in the leadership ranks needed money for their own PAC, to share with the campaigns of grateful colleagues.

At the meetings the lobbyists led their guests through halls bustling with activity. Then in a sumptuous conference room they showed a slick video about the client, whom the FBI had named CyberSolutions, and its interactive software that alerted company programmers to attempted hacking so they could provide rapid response. "We're the 'fire and forget' of defense systems protection," ran the tag line. "Put us on the case, so your team can focus on American security, not computer security." Black's bosses had picked this specialty on the advice of the agent-turned-lobbyist, who said that there was so much money being thrown at new approaches to cyber security that helping a company get funded to demonstrate feasibility wouldn't be difficult. An added benefit was that the targets would know that an exploratory contract in this growing area was not likely to spur challenges or complaints from established companies, like a contract for components of weapons would.

The lobbyists then said that the startup had 125 employees and family members who wanted to "max out" to the campaign, which meant each would write two $2,800 checks, one for the primary election and one for the general. Funds left over from the primary season, even if there was no opposition, could legally be rolled into the general election, so this was a pledge of an unrestricted $700,000. Some would also give the maximum permitted to the Member's PAC, which was $5,000, and to state party groups who would be supporting the campaign, for another $10,000. That would bring the total to at least a million dollars. And the CyberSolutions company itself was willing to give up to another million in its own funds to an "uncoordinated" PAC, if the race became difficult and one was created.

Now the dance began. The FBI lobbyists sat back and waited for the Members or their representatives to talk. Neither the money nor the pitch was unusual at this point. All that was unusual was that the FBI had a warrant and was taping the meeting.

Black's adviser, the former agent, had counseled patience at this point. Members faced this moment hundreds of times each election cycle, both in the money search and the vote search. They wanted someone's support and they generally agreed with the "ask," but for legal or political reasons knew they couldn't say or write words that openly committed to a particular action. Instead they relied on the situation to make their approval obvious. Especially with a lobbying firm, it would be understood that additional contributions would be based on fulfilling the initial unspoken commitment.

The former agent had told Black and her team: "One of my partners is a former House Member. He'd been a federal district attorney, and he'd always remind his congressional staff that he'd put a lot of people in prison because they'd written or said what they didn't need to. He told them, on everything from fundraising to legislation, to be like him and pretend that everything you said or wrote would end up on the front page of the New York Times. His rule was and still is, 'Never text or email what you can say on the phone, never say on the phone what you can say in person, and most important, never say in person what's already understood. Don't even wink if you can get by with a nod, and don't even nod if you don't have to.'

"The point is, when everybody knows what the deal has to be, don't stink up the room by affirming it. His favorite example was when he was invited on a presidential trip to Moscow, and was in the room when Bush, Putin, and the head of the World Bank reached an agreement in which billions in debt was deferred in exchange for a limit on oil production. It had sounded to him like a general discussion of world oil issues, but when he asked the World Bank staffer he was sitting next to what had just happened, she was able to tell him exactly how much debt and exactly how much oil had been agreed to. And both sides kept the bargain."

The Members and their campaign staff at first said all the safe things to the lobbyists, using careful words about how all companies need the chance to compete, and how the specialized staff in the congressional office would be glad to assist, as they would with any company, in identifying the right Pentagon or intelligence office to approach to find out about opportunities. Staying on script, the lobbyists responded noncommittally, and the meetings ended with polite promises to continue the discussion. After a month of waiting and a few desultory phone calls or emails with campaign staff who were "just checking in" on the company's plans, Jillian "Jilly" Krist, a subcommittee chair on House Armed Services, called one of the lobbyists and set up a one-on-one meeting. The hook had clearly caught, so Black asked the former agent to come in and help her "lobbyist" act out various scenarios for the upcoming meeting.

Congresswoman Krist was a white Democrat in a mostly black and Hispanic urban district that was safe from Republicans. However, the "rule or ruin" Justice Democrats had recently announced a black primary challenger, and Krist was determined not to become the next Joe Crowley, the white, senior House leader from a majority-minority district who'd been blindsided by a Hispanic woman in a low-turnout 2018 primary. That had been the first time since Berkeley councilman Ron Dellums defeated a long-time congressman in 1970 who was voting against the Vietnam war, but wasn't leading the charge, that a left-leaning Democrat had been taken down in a primary from the left. The congresswoman needed a lot of money to make sure it didn't happen to her.

In the meeting Krist tried to close the deal by bragging about how hard she had worked to help a clothing manufacturer who had been turned down by the Pentagon on a contract for millions of uniforms. "In the end, I just asked the chairman of the full committee to slide the entire uniform buy out of the defense bill and put in some report language on the need for an investigation of the foreign content percentage of the competitor's cloth. Since the firm was in my district, he knew I needed to show some fight. By the time the bill was ready for the floor a week later, the Pentagon asked the chairman to get a rule for an amendment to split the contract, and my company was mighty happy."

The lobbyist had been prepped for this type of pledge by comparison. "OK, so if CyberSecurity could do some significant subcontracting in your district, maybe set up one of our 200-person response offices there, you'd go to bat for us with the chairman if we bid on a contract and lose? Because then I think we'd be ready to give you this first cut right now." And with that she took off the top of her pile of papers a fat manila envelope that had been inspiring Krist's covetous looks throughout the meeting. She pulled out of it a stack of checks, all clipped together and plopped them on the table, between her and the congresswoman.

"That's 60 of the primary checks, $168,000, made out to your committee, with the federal information sheet attached to each. We'll spread the rest out over a couple of reporting periods. And let us know if things look tight and you set up a PAC for the company's money. They really want to help, and will really appreciate whatever you can do."

Krist didn't take the pile of checks. Instead she gave the lobbyist her finance manager's card and said, "You met John last time. Just messenger them to him."

The lobbyist stayed calm despite being certain that the agents in the taping room were high-fiving each other in victory. It wasn't a slam dunk, since the agent-actor rather than the target had made the crucial statement, but the act of accepting the contributions after the statement would probably hold up with a reasonable jury. Still, it wouldn't hurt to give Jilly Krist a bit more rope. There was no legal difference between grabbing the cash and telling how to direct it, but the grab would definitely have been better for a jury.

"Great, but I'm really curious about one thing, and I've got a lot to learn about this town. Off the record, can you tell me how you did it? What did you have to give the chairman to get the uniform buy pulled? I can tell you that in Kentucky that's not something that would just go into the favor bank. That kind of speed, late in the procurement process, that's probably rare around here, right?"

"Well, yes and no. It depends mostly on how badly the chairman wants something else." Krist relaxed too quickly after the tension of the negotiation, and launched into a bit more unnecessary bragging. "It was a classic, really. He didn't commit to the ask, just said he'd think about what he could do. Then as he politely escorted me out of his office with his old courtly manners, the way he always does for the ladies, he mentioned that he was worried about my sexual assault amendment gumming up the vote on final passage.

"Sexual assault in the military is my trademark issue, and I'd ridden the 'me too' movement into a successful committee vote appointing a Justice Department overseer for charging and clemency hearings. The services hate it; they say it destroys the chain of command, all that. But in this age of Harvey Weinstein and poor Al Franken every Democrat, even the chairman, had to vote for it. That was clearly the deal, so I sent my defense staffer over to talk to committee staff and soften the amendment to Sense of Congress, an opinion, not a requirement. I was gonna lose it in conference with the Senate anyway."

The Justice Department prosecutors were happy with that little bit of color. Along with some digging by Black's team, who produced some nice, fat numbers on Krist's contributions from the local uniform firm and its employees, it established a pattern of behavior that could only help in court.

While Black had been running the sting, her financial team had hit another jackpot. They had been sifting the records gathered with their subpoenas at the U.S. banks used by Mobe-Corp when out came a series of wire transfers from the same Delaware corporation used in the over-invoicing in the Niger arms deal. Digging deeper, they found that the transfers came during the weeks that employees and their families were writing personal checks to the 12 Members' campaigns. Even better, they found a slew of small bumps in salary checks to those employees in the next month, bumps that would add up over a year or so to the level of the contributions. It sure smelled like foreign funding of U.S. elections.

Black got approval for a raid on Mobe-Corp to cart away subpoenaed documents and access the mainframe directly from seized computers. Justice was confident that this would provide evidence for at least a corporate charge leading to a massive fine, and perhaps even felony charges for individuals. Any indictment for foreign interference in elections would add some buzz to a case that was proving to be a bit underwhelming: none of the other Members ever incriminated themselves like Representative Krist.

Krist's expected conviction for taking contributions in return for a promise of future assistance would pale beside the effect of Abscam's seven victories. Legal commentators would argue convincingly that case showed why it was essentially impossible to curtail the money chase, given the Supreme Court's consistent if contentious equation of campaign contributions with free speech. If just one of 12 fell for the sting, that meant the rest were doing fine without getting anywhere near the current border of illegality.

Even worse, before either the raid or Krist's indictment could take place, a vandal took the handle off Black's pump. Someone in the FBI leadership with a bone to pick with Wray leaked the sting story to the Washington Post, which ran it despite a meeting between the editor and the FBI director. The article also revealed that the sting related to Mobe-Corp's contributions to Members of Congress. That set off a flurry of activity among Mobe-Corp's top executives, who began to "lawyer up" with some of the Washington bar's most expensive talent.

The executives weren't too concerned about the minimal Federal Election Commission penalties for exceeding limits on contributions, and it was hard for prosecutors to prove that bonuses were direct compensation for campaign contributions. What they feared was that the FBI would find out that the rake-off from the arms deal hadn't just gone to covert operations overseas but also made its way back home, into elections. That was big stuff, felonies for money-laundering and conspiracy. Justice put people away for that. There'd be no presidential order of protection on this one. The investigation had to be stopped some other way, if possible.

CHAPTER 11:
APRIL 2021 – THE HIT

"We got him. We got him. The car tracker has Harris on the road to Bowling Green. You ready?" Shirley Tono's call found Black at her desk at four o'clock on a Tuesday afternoon. "We raid his house or wherever he goes first in DC, and VSP raids the renter's house at the same time. DC SWAT is settin' up on his house right now. If you want, you can meet us at the command post, the parking lot of the old Fletcher Johnson school. But you'll have to stay outside the perimeter when we go in."

Black was indeed eager to watch Cass and Tono walk out, in cuffs, the man who ordered Du'Shaunn's murder or maybe even carried it out. She signed out, and took her personal car, the Mustang. She figured it'd be safe in the midst of a hundred cops, and she didn't want to complicate her FBI life by taking an office beast on a personal case. Pulling into the steep parking lot off Benning Road, Black saw the heavy vehicles of the cavalry at the top and stopped dead. Mixed in with the DCPS jackets were some reading FBI.

Black called Tono. "What are my Fibbie peeps doing here? I can't be hanging with them." Cass, bulked up in a SWAT vest with a Kevlar helmet snapped on the front, walked down the parking lot to talk with her. "Sorry, McGurk, we just got here too," he explained. "You know DC, the feds have to be notified of any raid, and with federal gun charges on the table along with the local murder, sorry, your cousin's, they decided to send observers along."

"Wait," cut in Tono, who'd walked down to join them. "Here's the call." She turned up her hand-held radio and they listened as the Virginia state police reported to DC's undercover chase vehicles: "Suspect exited house with small knapsack, probably pistols. Driving north now on 301, brown old-style Cadillac, DC plates Paul Victor 3-7-6-5. Expect him over the bridge in 30 minutes. We're set up on the renter's house. We'll hold for your signal on the raid."

"OK," said Cass, "here's what we do. Everybody's waiting here until the undercover sees where Harris goes on the Terrace. Probably his house. Park your 'Stang over with the personal vehicles and we'll take you to the captain. She knows you've been helping us and she'll tell the Fibbies she's the one who asked you to come as an observer. So it's not on you. But remember, you're still outside the tape! Clear? Come grab a vest and helmet. That's protocol now, even for observers."

Two hours later, just as it was getting dark, the word came from the undercover officer, who was sitting in a ratty pickup down the street from Harris' house: he'd parked and covered the old Caddy and walked the bag up the street and into his house. "Mount up! Hats on, visors down, everybody, now!" DC patrol cars were radioed to pull onto the cross streets to block traffic and the convoy of six armored Lenco BearCat assault cars carrying the 24-man SWAT team hammered the mile down East Capitol to Clay Terrace in under a minute. The SWAT van carrying the equipment and the command staff lumbered not far behind on its LDV-modified Freightliner M55 chassis.

By the time neighborhood kids started yelling "5-0, 5-0" it was too late for anybody inside the house to run. The SWATs came from all four sides, without even bothering to tell the Kings to lie on the floor, far away from any weapons. The hunted knew the drill as well as the hunters. Nobody was getting out of this box.

As planned, Cass turned left off East Capitol, down 53rd Street against the one-way after the gleaming, massive new KIPP charter school, and then right, again against the one-way, onto Clay Terrace. He pulled onto a square asphalt playground between some projects on the terrace level, above Harris' house on Dix Street, to wait for the heavies to go in. Floodlights on the projects revealed women and girls gathered in doorways. The men and boys had all run down to watch the action as soon as they heard the shouts of 5-0. "Oh my Lord, we're right back where Makiyah Wilson was killed in 2018," Tono said. "Ten years old. Hey, it took us a year but we got 'em all, all four shooters and another eight helpin' out. 'Let's go do wat we do,' those idiot Wellington Park rascals texted before they gatted this whole square. Yeah, well, we went and did what we do too!"

The boom of a heavy metal door being smashed off its hinges interrupted her. "Here we go! McGurk, no closer than the street." Cass and Tono jumped out of the front seats and hurried across the projects toward the hill down to Dix Street. Black came more slowly out of the back seat, knowing she needed to lag behind a bit. They wouldn't bring anybody out until the house was fully secure, in maybe ten minutes. She felt kind of silly, standing in a playground in a full burka, as everybody called the new helmet, looking out through the eye slit at a bunch of little girls looking back at her. So she started walking too.

Suddenly, a Jeep Cherokee came squealing into the square from between two of the projects. Time stood still for Black as she watched it pull broadside, just 20 yards away, with the stubby barrels of Tech-9s sticking out of the front and back windows. She instinctively threw her arms up over her head and started to duck, just as a stream of bullets slammed into her and shredded the windows of the cop car. It was over in five seconds. Stunned by the noise of the firing and the exploding glass, Cass and Tono never even drew their guns until the Cherokee had bounded away over a curb onto 53rd and headed south.

* * *

The FBI swarmed into action, and the MPD, from top to bottom, didn't negotiate or slow-walk the feds up and down its chain of command as they usually did. Cass and Tono put out the word that this was their girl, and everybody was eager to play nice. Within an hour an FBI task force of 100 had been selected and given a direct line to any MPD units they wanted.

6-D found the Cherokee within minutes behind the Shrimp Boat, abandoned and wiped clean. It had been stolen in Prince George's County the night before. FBI canvassing teams blanketed the areas around the shooting and the car, accompanied by the officers who usually patrolled those places. The size and vigor of the effort disarmed a lot of the usual resistance to cooperation. Cameras on the playground confirmed what residents said: the attack was carried out by four black men who were wearing sports jackets and black gloves and had their baseball caps pulled low. At the Shrimp Boat they had simply walked away, disappearing into side streets and alleys. Whether by coincidence or design, there were no cameras covering where they'd left the car or where they'd walked.

The shooters all seemed to be in their late 20s and early 30s, definitely not teenagers like most of the known Clay Kings. The MPD told the FBI that this meant the hit was probably a contract or an exchange of favors, carried out by a gang from another city. DC gangs usually wanted to take credit for drive-bys, to make a point, but for special hits like witnesses they sometimes went to people who really knew how to get the job done.

Three days later, just after the director finished his obligatory visit, the agent in charge of the task force came into Black's hospital room with his top lieutenants. She had never met Bob DeWitt, but she'd heard stories. He was a top dog, number one on the hit parade of the "blowtorches," the senior agents who were too rough-edged to get on the ladder to the directorship, and didn't want to anyway. Blowtorches were well past running regional offices. They formed a bullpen ready to run big cases, like this assassination attempt.

"Agent McGurk, I'm Agent DeWitt. I've been told to solve both your shooting and the possibly related murder of Mr. Du'Shaunn Ruff. First of all, it's good to see you alive and kicking. 103 shells at the scene, 10 bullets in your vest, six marked your helmet, and four found your arms and legs. The doctors tell me some of those wounds will stay with you, but you're still one lucky lady. Now, are you ready to talk, or do we have to get some B.S. lawyer in here?"

Black had thought about that question as soon as she came out of the haze of the operations. Nobody could ever formally fault her for taking advantage of her right to a union lawyer during all questioning relating to the use of force, or to the misuse of FBI resources, if her little gambit at Quantico came out. But she suspected it would smell bad for her career if she held anything back and tried to pull what the Bureau derisively called a "Ben Bradlee," parceling out only the bits she wanted to.

In 1964 the famed Washington Post editor, lionized during the Watergate affair for castigating officials for lying and withholding evidence, had taken it upon himself to decide that his sister-in-law's diary about her romantic ties to President Kennedy had no bearing on her murder. He lied about the diary's existence and the CIA's search for it during the investigation and the murder trial, depriving both prosecution and defense of vital information.

No, Black wasn't going down that road. She'd decided to play it straight with the bureau and trust the big shots to let her personal use of Quantico resources slide. Her main goal, anyway, was to see Du'Shuann's murderer caught. DeWitt, not she, had the case. He was the one who had to figure out what was relevant and what wasn't. "Let's get all these rascals. I'm an open book, to you and your team. Hit me."

DeWitt had clear instructions from the director. Solve the case quickly, while the public still had its eye on the attempted assassination, so that everybody would know that harming an agent is a guaranteed suicide mission. He could make deals in minutes that would usually take months, without even consulting the Justice prosecutors. After pumping Black for a day, DeWitt's team laid it out to James Harris and his lawyer, prominent DC defense attorney Sharia Denby, whose guarantee of payment was six mortgages for properties Harris owned through relatives. They could put him away forever on the guns, but if he became the one smart soul who gave them the entire plot to kill Agent McGurk, he'd do some two years of safe time in isolation and then win the free pass, Witness Protection with all the trimmings. Oh, and he had one minute to decide before they moved on to other Kings.

"We don't even need that much time," replied Denby. "James is gonna give you everything right now, because I know you're in a hurry. We can work out the Protection details later; I've worked with Bob before and I know he'll appreciate our help. But I've got to warn you first, you're not going to be happy with some of what James has to give, because you're barking up the wrong tree. You're going to get the truth today, but it won't solve your cases, either of them, the agent or the teenager with the jacket. You still want to make the trade?"

The FBI still did, and Harris laid it out. He said he was first among equals in the "Famous Five" at the top of the Kings, the main shot-caller and the day-to-day operations man for drugs. He proved it by giving up the three renters the Kings used in addition to the guy in Bowling Green.

"Look, I'd know if a King be even hintin' on takin' out a cop, let alone a fed, 'specially 'cause we Five talked on what to do when we hear she be pokin' 'round, likin' us for jackin' her cousin. And what we decided to do was nothin', 'cause we wasn't good for it. Bank: nobody axed for no shot on no Du'Shaunn Ruff, and nobody called none."

Harris admitted that "somebody" had checked with "somebody" in CIU and found out that they thought the kid Ruff had fought at HD was a King. And when the FBI asked, he even gave up the somebodies. But Gangs was wrong: yeah, the kid had run for them back when he was 14, and yeah, he hadn't snitched, but there were dozens of kids like that. That didn't make them Kings. When he came out of juvie his mom moved him to North Carolina for a year, and after that he'd kept his distance. They could care less if he got his ass kicked. In fact, Harris had never even heard about the fight, or knew who Black's cousin was. Kings never went over to Simple City.

When the FBI squeezed him on Tupelo Jones, who had traded the Jackie Robinson jacket, Harris said he was indeed a full-blood King, a mid-level man, but that he'd been pulled back after their source told them that CIU was looking to run him in for Cass and Tono. If he'd been involved in taking out Ruff, he never told Harris about it. And Harris had never seen him in a Jackie Robinson jacket either, that was for sure. Since he was risking his life to get off the gun charge and into Witness Protection, giving up renters and an MPD source, and would lose it all for a single lie, the agents were pretty sure he was being straight on Jones. Denby's reputation was almost a guarantee of that.

Things moved pretty quickly from there. The McGurk assassination no longer looked like a gang hit, which left the uncomfortable conclusion that it was related to her work, probably the FedEx probe. Mobe-Corp too was capable of rustling up hitters, and that was where the investigation had to go. On the Ruff murder, all four of Harris' renters got immunity, yet still swore they hadn't been the source of the gun. So the FBI went back to Jerome Cleaveland, the shooter in the Alexandria jail, and dragged the county DA in to make it clear to Cleaveland that he would indeed serve his full five years, no matter how much this reneging on a deal screwed up plea-bargaining on other cases. He would also be called to a grand jury with immunity on gun trafficking.

Then DeWitt took over for the unhappy prosecutor, laying it out for Cleaveland's lawyer. "If he refuses to talk then it won't be just contempt of court, but obstruction of justice in protecting a suspect in a case involving the attempted assassination of an FBI agent. I want it all on the renter and I want it now."

And he got it. That legal theory of obstruction, as the lawyer strenuously pointed out, was nonsense, but the FBI could hold on to Cleaveland for the years it would take to fight it out in court. Cass whispered to Tono, as they sat there in amazement at the difference between their resources and the FBI's, "Jesus Christ, this ain't even fair. They don't have to do any work!"

Cleaveland's renter wasn't on the list provided by James Harris, which suggested that Tupelo Jones had indeed gone off by himself on the Ruff murder. When the FBI picked the renter up, he didn't even ask for Witness Protection. He was glad to give up his clients and the gun in exchange for immunity. "Sure, I'll testify. 'Bout time I left this business anyway. And I'm not scared of them. Just a bunch of kids. It wasn't no NFL business—just shopping. I asked the young bloods and they didn't dare tell me different, 'cause I would've checked with the OGs."

CHAPTER 12:
MAY-DECEMBER 2021 – SHOPPING

Cass and Tono brought the transcript of the interview with Tupelo Jones over to Georgetown Hospital, where Black was lounging in the Intensive Care Unit even though it was two weeks after surgery. She was supposed to have been moved out of the orbit of the highest quality nurses five days ago, but this was the FBI: there was no expense spared for a wounded agent. A pair of State Department security agents sat at her door, the result of an offer from the Secretary of State. When you care enough, you send the very best, and State cared a lot about its relations with the FBI, which had been strained to the breaking point by the FedEx Files.

Jones had told the sad tale of Du'Shauun's death, of course from a perspective minimizing his own role in it. There was no international intrigue here, not even any dramatic gang retaliation. Just the same old senseless nihilism and pathetic stupidity of black underclass teenage life that Cass and Tono dealt with daily, and that Black had lived. Just shopping.

That's the street synonym for strong-arm robbery that an 18-year-old friend of 17-year-old Tupelo Jones had used when he texted him that fateful Friday night 15 months before: "shoping?" He was a senior in a Prince George's high school, a Jamaican, from one of the highest-achieving academic cultures, and he couldn't even spell that right. They agreed to meet at Gallery Place at 9. The PG kid brought along a 16-year-old cousin who ran with him in the NFL— Niggaz from Landover. The cousins had been to Gallery Place before to fight, answering a social media challenge from a DC gang, but this time it was going to be all fun and profit. The younger cousin's only concern had been for his new basketball shoes: "We need ta beam somebody, you do the first punch, mon. I can't be having blood on these— it don't never wash out. You lay'm down, I come in behind and kick the body."

Ruff just happened to be on the same metro car Jones rode to Gallery Place. As the train pulled in, Jones saw Ruff take the Robinson jacket out of his backpack and put it on. Smart boy, thought Jones, keeping that out of sight east of the river. But not smart enough. He followed Ruff as he left the station and walked over to the food court, texting with the cousins all the way. The deed was as good as done. The older cousin drove off to a renter the NFL had a number for, and Jones and the younger cousin tracked Ruff as he flirted with girls, ate at Chipotle, and eventually headed home with a friend.

Ruff put the jacket back in his backpack as they rode into the Minnesota Avenue station, and he and the friend went off on separate buses. Alerted by text, the older cousin was waiting with the car and the gun, and they followed the V8 bus along Benning Road until Ruff got off at the old Fletcher Johnson school and walked a block to 46th Street, at the bottom of the hill up to Benning Heights— Simple City. They followed with the lights off as he walked up to the ball field on the ridge, at F Street, and started to cross it. It was time. They rushed out of the car and the older cousin punched Ruff to the ground. The others joined in, kicking, and grabbing at the backpack. But Du'Shaunn wouldn't give it up, so the older cousin showed him the gun. Instead of giving the jacket up, went Jones' tale, Ruff rushed them and got shot. "Nobody wanted nobody shot. That was the plan— show him the gun and he gives it up."

Black asked the detectives, "How much of this nonsense do you believe?" They shrugged their shoulders. There was nothing to say. Jones had the best lawyer of the three, and he'd made sure Jones told the first story that worked. So Jones was the one who got to plead to a light sentence, probably five for robbery, out in two. Based on statements by Jones and the renter, the older cousin had been indicted for first degree murder while armed. The younger cousin had been indicted as an adult for second-degree felony murder.

The cousins could plead to lesser charges and do close to 20 and 10 years, respectively, or they could risk an additional ten years each for a conviction at trial. The case was as solid as a rock. And it didn't hurt that they were the children of immigrants, and lived in PG County. A few "nullifiers" popped up every year on DC juries who simply refused to "send yet another of our young black men to prison" despite overwhelming evidence of horrific violence. But they'd be less tempted to make this protest against "mass incarceration" for some PG kids, Jamaicans at that.

"So that's that," concluded Tono. "We're gonna go by your grandmother's today, lay it all out. And we'll keep you in the loop as much as you want as it goes forward. But how about your case, this hit?"

Just then the State security guy knocked on the door. "Hey, your girlfriend's here. How long should I tell her?"

"Oh, send her in," replied Black. "We're done. I'll call you guys, bring you up to date when I know more on the hit. They're keeping me in the dark, just like I'd do. Classic FBI!"

* * *

After a month in the hospital, Black was sent home for two months of daily intense physical therapy for the reconstructed nerves in her right, shooting arm. The pain was remarkable, but the PT kept insisting that strengthening now would dramatically reduce the "cold morning" pain in later years. She'd be able to do most things right-handed, but nothing stressful, like fire a weapon, throw a punch, or even manhandle a suspect.

Her street days were over, but as Director Wray said, it was about time she moved up to the management track. He called her his "golden girl," at 32 ready to lead a regional office, the stepping stone to senior DC positions. He recommended El Paso, the border region. "El Paso's high risk, high reward: you'll be part of the effort to block illegal immigration, which the Democrats and their mainstream media demonize, but arresting nasty human traffickers is feel-good stuff, even to them. And any job you take is going to be publicized: your head's way above the parapet now anyway, since you're one of the few FBI agents the media and so the public know by name.

"At this point you're a symbol, and you're never gonna please everybody, not even the black Members of Congress. They'll push for you, but always with their eyes on what the Black Lives Matter crowd is saying about law enforcement, let alone the lies the AOCs are saying about the border. Look what happened to Senator Harris: her greatest asset was that she could appeal to the political middle in a general election as a tough prosecutor, but that became her greatest liability with the left in the primaries. But anyway, what do you think?"

Naomi had convinced Black that she should stop hiding her weakness with middle class references. So she told the director: "Well, sir, what I mostly think is what the hell is a parapet? Tell me that and I'll take any job you like!"

While she was in rehab, Black's three separate investigations ground on: the hit, the sting, and the underlying FedEx corruption case. DeWitt worked the hit aggressively, raiding Mobe-Corp, seizing all its employment records and emails. His team identified two African-American contractors, former Army Special Forces, whose passports in and out of the country fit the time frame of the hit. However, the office records showed that both were on a long-planned, regular two-week rotation for home leave, and both had alibis, complete with receipts, for other activities in other cities during the actual hit. There were no cameras in those places, though.

It was on the foreign side that DeWitt's efforts really broke down. The CIA self-investigated its connections to the contractors and reported none at all. Wray protested the FBI's inability to interview CIA agents, but the president turned him down. Wray sort of understood that: he would have resigned before he'd have let the CIA talk to his people, at home or abroad. When DeWitt came in to talk privately with Wray about the status of the investigation, the blowtorch didn't mince words.

"OK, so the CIA erected a wall. Asking them for help is like punching a marshmallow. We'll never get a straight story or even a single bit of credible evidence out of them. So I'm not going to solve this case, but that doesn't mean we can't send the message you wanted sent, that nobody takes out an FBI agent with impunity. I know just how to send that message to the country and to the CIA, and I know the only person who can approve it.

"You need to talk, alone, with the president. We're owed that. Tell the president that if this were Israel, or Russia, or China, or even France, these two Mobe-Corp thugs would be grabbed, tortured to talk, and disappeared along with whomever they gave up.

"Those countries don't believe in coincidences when it comes to their people, and neither should we. Look at the Israelis after Munich in '72, and the Soviet Alpha force in Lebanon after the 1985 kidnapping by Hezbollah. And just last year the Russians struck again, taking out a former Chechen commander out for a stroll in a park in Berlin. Blood on the tracks, balls in their mouths. If there's some collateral damage, the message is still delivered, and in some ways even enhanced.

"Remind the president that you and I both know, and indeed lots of people in Congress know, that after 9/11 we asked a couple of those countries to do us that sort of favor, to protect our citizens. Well, why the hell can't we ask again, on behalf of our agents? They'd be only too glad to put that in the favor bank. Get me the go-ahead, and all it'll take me is just some winks and nods with our friends. The President's clean, you're clean, and I'm a tomb. And if we get anything, maybe it jumpstarts the investigation again."

Wray put his hands up to stop DeWitt, and lectured him harshly. "Are you crazy, even thinking that, even joking about something like that out loud? And I know you're joking, out of frustration. There's not even gonna be a Comey-like memo for the files on this meeting. As far as I'm concerned, you and I talked, realized that the investigation has hit a dead end, and agreed the best we can do is ask the president to bar Mobe-Corp from government business. The case goes to the Emmett Till unit, where it shall forever languish. It hurts me too, but all we can do is help McGurk move onward and upward.

"Jesus, Bob, you are a blunt instrument. You know so much history, the '70s this, the '80s that, so go look at the trouble Ronald Reagan and Elliott Abrams got into, asking other countries to do our business to get around the laws about notifying Congress." And then he winked at DeWitt, ever so quickly, and nodded, ever so slightly.

As for the sting, Congresswoman Jillian Krist did become the warning to others that the Justice Department wanted. There was, of course, disappointment at the FBI that there were no "others" from the 11 in the pipeline with her. Krist declined the "Agnew option," named after Vice President Spiro Agnew, and turned down an implicit offer to resign in exchange for the charges being dropped. Then, like many Members before her, she was re-elected while under indictment. After conviction, though, the jig was up.

First Speaker Pelosi suspended Krist from all of her committees and all of her party leadership positions. Then the House Ethics Committee investigated the case and unanimously recommended expulsion. As was its tradition, the Committee did not simply cite the result of the court case but rather examined and made a judgment on the underlying evidence. Indeed, one of the House Members who would be sitting in judgment on the floor, Alcee Hastings, had himself been impeached, convicted, and removed as a federal judge despite being acquitted in a criminal trial for bribery. At this point, Krist resigned and served a two-year prison sentence.

Attorney General Barr's decision to brief and trust the big four and the House and Senate counsels before the sting paid off. When the operation was revealed after Krist's indictment and arrest, there was no reprise of the Abscam anger and recourse to the courts. The Speaker's remarks were typical of those of the other leaders: "We were, properly, informed of an investigation, but not, again properly, of which Members were the targets. We stated our disagreement with the methods, the sting approach, but because the tactics did not impinge on the legislature's constitutional domain we did not have a basis to appeal the decision to the President. We will let the judicial process take its course."

As for the FedEx Files case itself, the original sin that started it all, Justice indicted 20 Nigeriens, based on the work of Black's task force. The Lion did not allow the legal attachés to question them, but he guaranteed personally to the American ambassador that the government employees had been fired and that the private business people were barred from any government contracts or participation in the offsets. In return, Justice agreed with a State Department request not to waste time and diplomatic capital seeking extraditions.

The lower-level Mobe-Corp employees who had sneaked onto the gravy train pled guilty to misdemeanors and paid fines. Two mid-level executives were charged with felonies for coordinating the foreign election donations, but the government was "gray-mailed" into dropping the case after they showed the judge, in a secret session, documents they intended to use that showed CIA and DOD use of the bank accounts.

All that remained to be determined was the fate of the arms deal. With the sting and then the assassination attempt, Mary Magdalen Carter and the FedEx coalition had been able to revive the effort that had been stymied by the AIA the previous year. And in December their amendment was one of the last items in the House-Senate conference committee negotiations on the Continuing Resolution, which funded the government's budget for the next year.

"Wait for some bodies to turn up" was a congressional maxim, coined by a liberal congressman in 1986 when he was asked by human rights groups when he would offer an amendment barring aid to the government of El Salvador. In that case, the congressman was right: the bodies that turned up in 1989 were those of six Jesuit priests slaughtered by the U.S.-backed Army, and the subsequent vote cut off military aid and effectively ended the war.

In the FedEx case, the bodies were those of Congresswoman Krist and especially Agent Mar'Shae McGurk. The FedEx coalition asked its congressional champions to add an amendment to the CR suspending the Spooky deal until the shooters in the assassination had been brought to justice and the president certified that none of the offset funds in Niger had "expressly or impliedly" been used to influence an American election. It added a permanent ban on any U.S. government contracting with Mobe-Corp.

To Carter's surprise and delight the House passed the amendment on a party line vote. The specter of continuing with a deal that had led to an assassination attempt on an FBI agent was too strong even for the Freedom from Terror campaign to counter. With elections every two years and primary challenges for insufficient purity currently being a "Squad" and not just a Tea Party practice, it was just too risky for House Democrats to vote "no."

But when the Democrats' foreign aid appropriator, Patrick Leahy, offered the same amendment in the Senate— where Members are elected for six long years in which lots of sins can be not just forgiven but forgotten— it was rejected by all the Republicans and half of the Democrats.

The legendary advocacy group for military aid to Israel, AIPAC, had argued to Democrats that the amendment created a dangerous precedent for applying impossible corruption standards to countries other than Niger— like Israel, with its history of bribery charges against prime ministers. While anti-Israel sentiment was weak, or at least hidden, among House Democrats, with less than ten percent opposing a bill denouncing the Boycott, Divest and Sanctions movement, it was non-existent among their Senate colleagues.

And so to conference, in an ornate cubbyhole of a room off the Senate floor. Here the advocates of the Niger deal didn't talk or even think about Israel. Here there was no posturing about saving Africans from terrorism. Here the administration's chosen tactic was to force the conferees to look America's role in the world squarely in the face.

The media and the public were allowed to attend the conference, but there was really little point to waiting in line to squeeze in. Every disagreement that was more than a matter of differing technical language or funding levels was resolved in private discussions, and its resolution was simply announced to and approved by the conferees. It was easier just to wait for the appropriations staff to send out the summary for conferees when it ended. By midnight, when the conference got to its last two outstanding issues— Niger's arms deal and a House provision eliminating the emergency powers that President Trump had used two years before to fund the southern border wall— only a few people from the press and interest groups remained.

The two issues were informally paired because Pelosi had made it clear to Majority Leader McConnell that the House was going to need a total of one win on them: half a loaf on each or a full loaf on one. To open discussion on the House's Niger amendment, the leading Senate Democrat on the conference asked Admiral F. D. Kirtland, the Chief of Naval Operations, to explain the administration's position.

As is usually the case with naval strategists since Captain Alfred Thayer Mahan lectured and wrote in the 19th century on *The Influence of Seapower upon History*, there was no room in the Chief's cold-eyed case for the patriotic bombast and weeping humanitarianism to which ground commanders, who actually see casualties, gravitate. A Marine general would have led off with: "The sound of an AC-130 hovering over station? That's the sound of freedom." An Army general would have recounted how AFRICOM troops risk their lives, and in Niger had actually laid them down, to save African lives, with mobile clinics to inoculate children and night patrols to safeguard villagers from terrorists.

None of that stuff for the Chief, who explained that America only dominated the global political and economic space because it demonstrated daily that it dominated the global battle space. Imperial strategists from the Peloponnesian Wars, the Roman Republic, the Ming Dynasty, and the European colonial era would have approved of his honesty. Speaking from notes, but pausing to look intently at the Members as he spoke, Kirtland he made the case for the sale.

"To quote that great American, Bob Dylan, 'Let us not talk falsely now, the hour is getting late.' Fighting corruption, backing human rights and democracy, yes, those are important American values. And we in the armed forces, just like you in the Congress, try to promote those in whatever we do. But those are complex goals, ever-sought but never perfected in partner nations with unique and sometimes contradictory conditions. These goals must be pursued in the context of our national interest. And our national interest, unique among all other nations today— an exceptional national interest, to use that word in the most positive way— is also the international interest.

"In this historical moment, ever since the changing of the guard as the Europeans lost their colonial grip after World War II, we have replaced them as the guardian of the international interest. And so we have guaranteed the stable, free-flowing world economy that since the end of World War II has given all countries dramatically higher income and given all their people dramatically longer life expectancy. And by the way, for all the Europeans' moaning about us backing dictators today, don't forget that they lost their empires grudgingly, fighting all the way, asking us take them back after the war to French Indochina, Dutch Indonesia, British Malaysia, Portuguese Southern Africa, and arm them in the liberation wars that resulted.

"Now I'm not going to talk mawkishly, like General Powell did as secretary of state, about how much we have given in lives and treasure to be the guardian of others' interests. He said we do all this 'to put down oppression…in the interests of preserving the rights of people,' and that 'the only land we ever asked for was enough land to bury our dead.' Well, yes, in most cases we did indeed manage to help others. But in other cases it was, and it has to be, the opposite. When I hear my Army colleagues greet each other with their Green Beret motto of 'free the oppressed,' I always joke, 'or oppress the free, whatever it takes to get the job done.'

"And that job is our national interest in being the dominant global power. We don't do it for others. We do it for ourselves. Our prosperity, our opportunity, comes from our dominant role in the world. And that starts, that is guaranteed by, our dominant military role, in technology, in fighting capability, and— and this is the main point in your decision tonight— in allies who cooperate, quickly and fully, with the basing and intelligence we need to maintain our dominance."

The Chief paused, saw that the Members were riveted by this rare truth-telling, and plunged on: "What's the world's currency? The dollar, so that other countries will hold our debt, and let us print the money we need to be secure. Who benefits the most from world economic growth? We do, because a share of every profit, anybody's, goes to demand for our goods and services and corporations and universities. And what does an arms sale to Niger have to do with this? Everything. This is where we show that we stand with, we reward, we respect our allies in this great struggle for stability and order. This is the glue that holds our power together.

"Human rights and democracy, good government, less corruption, tolerance for differences on religion, sexual orientation, and other personal rights…all these do tend to come in the wake of stability and order, although not always in an immediate, direct fashion. But to have a wake, you need a ship, and in this case an aircraft carrier, a guided missile destroyer, a submarine, a landing ship. And yes, I'm speaking somewhat metaphorically, so add in your favorite Army, Air Force, and Marine gear, and your global satellite, audio surveillance, and communication networks.

"So we are an empire, the empire, protecting the stability of the world's economy from disruption. Sea lanes, access to the fuels and strategic minerals that modern economies and armed forces must have yet often don't like to produce, and access to markets. Those are the reasons why Admiral Perry and the Navy first plowed into Tokyo Bay in 1853. And those are the reasons why we patrol the South China Sea and the Strait of Hormuz today.

"Now as historical empires go, we're pretty benign. Most countries look to us to maintain this peace that lets the world grow. And make no mistake about it: most Americans support our military and its effort to maintain our position as the world's leader. They're no different from what citizens were like in ancient Rome, rapacious Sweden, colonial Britain, or imperial Japan. Power is popular.

"We held firm against the Soviet effort to be the empire, and now we hold firm against two very different efforts, radical Islam and China. Nature abhors a vacuum, and if you think we have to make some compromises to maintain our network of cooperation with feudal regimes, with homophobic ones, with corrupt ones, just think whether the mullahs, or China, care at all about the behavior of their client regimes.

"It's going to be a hundred years before governments develop in the Islamic world, from Indonesia to North Africa, that can truly be called democracies. This bizarre fundamentalism in people's minds about women, about tolerating other religions and opinions, has to be worn down by the modern world, by modern generations. What do we do in the meantime? Cede the field to our enemies and competitors?

"The Obama administration faced this choice when General Sisi overthrew the elected president, Morsi, in Egypt. It was clearly a coup, an undemocratic act, but most people on the ground agreed that Morsi was creating a theocracy himself and assisting, not reporting, terrorists. Obama chose the ally who would cooperate with us on chasing terrorists, no questions asked, no delay. The same choice is clear for us today: more Saudi Arabias or more Irans. One allies with us militarily and economically, one is at war with us.

"A political scientist recently wrote a book saying that there are Turkeys and Eagles when it comes to our foreign policy. He was referring to Benjamin Franklin's effort to make our national symbol the stay-at-home wild turkey, not the wandering, rapacious bald eagle. Turkeys reject the compromises that are needed to maintain dominance, preferring to ally only with well-behaved democracies. In fact they probably, in their hearts, oppose forward projection of U.S. military power, period.

"But as the author noted, there are very few Turkeys in Congress; most Democrats are Soft Eagles, pushing for dominance with a blend of human rights and democracy, but they are Eagles nonetheless just like the Hard Eagle Republicans. Johnson, Carter, Clinton, and Obama were just as much a part of the consensus for military dominance, power projection, and determining the makeup of governments in the formerly colonial countries as Nixon, Reagan, and the Bushes. What we in the Pentagon call 'the long war' for control of the Islamic world is formally called 'the war on terror' only because the Islamists, as Bin Laden openly said, attacked us as 'the far enemy' who maintained their true enemy, the Saudi regime, in power. We were fighting the long war long before Bin Laden, and we're fighting long after he's gone. Thanks, Navy Seals, by the way.

"Now we all remember Lee Hamilton, that liberal but pragmatic Congressman. I heard him tell a meeting of Members just like this in 2008 that was considering cutting off arms to the Saudis over their admittedly atrocious human rights record: 'Sorry. We just have to do it, ally with them. Period. The stakes, the oil, the military access, are just too high to take a risk.' So, please, tonight, find a way to send a message of support for anti-corruption without breaking an alliance that gives us drone bases we need, with a leader who dared to march against the Islamists in Paris. He's on our side. It's a war. Like Lee Hamilton said, we have to do it. Period."

The Democratic senator now spoke. "Thank you, Admiral Kirtland. Now, let's look at the situation on the ground. As the Chief said, we need allies, and you don't keep them if you don't support them. Niger has done us straight in the war on terror, giving us not just these drone bases but immediate and full cooperation and intelligence-sharing. We have to think of the effect that blocking the deal will have not just on this Lion in our corner, but on what the Saudis and other allies in the Middle East will think. We have a letter here from 15 former secretaries of state and defense, both parties, telling us we need to keep the sale going, to maintain our credibility in the broader region.

"Now I've prepared a substitute amendment, which addresses the corruption problems revealed by the FedEx Files. This is a more appropriate response to the situation than an attempt to use the tragedy of the attack on Agent McGurk to disrupt our alliance with the democratic government of Niger. My amendment releases the arms funding in tranches, based on quarterly reporting on progress made in ending corruption in the Defense Ministry. And the administration has told me it will accept this amendment, along with a ban on Mobe-Corp participating in any way in the Niger deal. Boeing has agreed to take on its tasks and its offsets, and as you all know there's been no implication of wrong-doing by Boeing in this matter."

At this point the main House sponsor of the amendment was called upon to speak. She was not on the conference committee, but the Speaker had asked that she be called in as the advocate. She started politely: "With all respect to the Admiral, this is not about Turkeys and Eagles, about whether America's allies will keep working with us if we take a stand against corruption, about how we'll lose our bases, rights and cooperation around the world and have to come home while China soars into our place. Please. This is about corruption, pure and simple; this is about people thinking they can assassinate FBI agents with impunity, pure and simple. This is about our values, not some referendum on our foreign policy."

"I've been hearing these sorts of apocalyptic things about damaging our foreign policy, our national interest, since I was a staffer here during the fight in the 1980s to get the Reagan administration to respect human rights and democracy. Chief, I personally heard one of your predecessors make the same arguments in the same conference committee about why we had to keep backing the Marcos dictatorship. Paul Wolfowitz, who was running Asia for Reagan at that time, was no different from Richard Holbrooke running it for Carter before him: 'Our Pacific fleet will collapse without our bases in the Philippines. We just have to do it, despite his human rights abuses.'

"Well, we didn't accept his expert opinion, and Congress started dialing back on support for Marcos. Benigno Aquino came back, and after his assassination his wife won the election. Marcos disappeared and things worked out just fine. Yes, it's true that a rent dispute with the democratic government closed the base for a while, but the world didn't end, and we're back there again with our ships. And I note that we also dock for repairs at Cam Ranh Bay in Vietnam. Friends and allies can change, but the US

Navy is still in the waters of East Asia. Our military plans can always survive a change of bases; our reputation as a beacon for human rights and democracy, which is our most valuable asset in global strategy, can't take backing corruption and assassination.

"Administrations always make these catastrophic predictions and never learn the lesson when they don't happen. Hey, Wolfowitz went right off to be ambassador to Indonesia after Marcos finally fell, and immediately started making the same case for military support for Suharto, the dictator there. It's been the same since Diem and Thieu and all the Vietnamese regimes, since Carter backed Siad Barre in Somalia in exchange for military bases, creating a 40-year disaster of a civil war that continues to today.

"So I'm tired of hearing from all these former government officials, coordinated on their letter by Boeing, I'm sure. Citing their titles is just another *ad hominem* argument, and their tired reasoning about credibility with dictators is exactly what started wars in Vietnam, Angola, Central America, Afghanistan, and dozens of places and kept them going long after they were lost.

"Government official don't have a monopoly on foreign policy facts or wisdom. Never have, never will. The Chief mentioned Colin Powell, who held the most prestigious military and diplomatic positions in our country. Well, there turned out to be literally not one true claim in the dozens he made in his speech to the United Nations making the case for an invasion of Iraq for having weapons of mass destruction. And his speech was based on the expert opinion of the CIA and the rest of our giant intelligence bureaucracy! Millions of Iraqis died because Members of Congress believed that the CIA wouldn't lie.

"Does nobody pay a price in our government for failure, or do we just let them feed us the same line all over again? I know my party has been mooning over intelligence and military analysts lately, because we like what they've said about Russian interference in our elections and the threat of climate change, but let's not forget how wrong, how politicized, and how dangerous their assessments can be."

"Now, it's time to put a stop to all this, to take a clear position: no arms to corrupt, repressive regimes. It violates our values, it creates the very military conflicts our forces end up being drawn into, conflicts that devastate and result in millions dying of disease and starvation when society breaks down. If we can't take a stand against this when we see the arrogance of arms dealers who think they can try to assassinate an FBI agent, we'll never take a stand on anything.

"Congress was finally shocked into doing the right thing in Central America at the end of the 1980s, when the slaughter of Jesuit priests in El Salvador and of rural Indians in Guatemala, both by forces trained and armed by us, led to a cut in aid to their armies. The result was peace and democracy, in both countries. Let's take the same stand today, shocked by the assassination attempt on Mar'Shae McGurk."

The discussion was desultory at that point, and actually moot, because as the Chief was speaking, the two managers had cut a deal and confirmed it with calls to Pelosi and McConnell. The House would get a $100 million cap on the president's emergency authority to raid Pentagon accounts, and the Senate would get the arms deal with a few reporting requirements. The Lion and his general would get their Magic Dragons, and the CIA would keep its new base.

So in the end Boeing, the AIA, and their Committee to Defend Africa prevailed. Like the NFL kids who killed Du'Shaunn Ruff, they too had gone "shopping," looking for arms deals, easy money in a violent world, and gotten away with it. Boeing received permission in a one-time agreement with the Department of Justice to hire the entire Mobe-Corp crew that was already on the ground. Mobe-Corp itself was out of the Niger deal, but it continued to get other government contracts.

Under pressure from Members of Congress with large universities in their districts, the Nigerien students got to keep their AID scholarships. There was an understanding that somebody had to pay, though, and the wheel of misfortune landed on the AID administrator, who resigned under a House threat of reduced funding. Mary Magdalen Carter and the African working group went on to other challenges, the empire went on dominating, and Special Agent in Charge Mar'Shae "Black" McGurk went on to El Paso.

ACKNOWLEDGMENTS

There would be no Mar'Shae McGurk thrillers without my wonderful students who were unfairly shackled by the nonsensical curriculum and phony grades at Washington DC's H. D. Woodson, Friendship Tech Prep, and Duke Ellington high schools. I hope that "Black" reflects just a bit of their verve, challenges, and potential. I love you guys.

My thanks go to the many people who were generous with their time and expertise as I developed this plot. Bill Hartung of the Center for International Policy knows arms transfers and offsets. His long career explaining U.S. arms transfer policy to the public meant I could leave that field in 2000 and the public wouldn't miss a thing.

Tom Cardamone of Global Financial Integrity knows transfer pricing and corruption. He's been my ally on so many issues, like the campaign to ban landmines and the "No Arms to Dictators" arms trade Code of Conduct.

From his many years at the Aerospace Industries Association Joel Johnson knows how weapons deals are made and approved. He beat me in 1992 on F-15s to Saudi Arabia with USA Jobs Now, and he was kind not to gloat as we recalled it.

The emeritus dean of American University's School of International Service, Lou "Green Dean" Goodman, has for 20 years counseled and consoled me. Many academics talk about defending the rights of scholars with whom they disagree on various issues. Lou just does it. He kindly provided his perspective on American University's involvement with Nigerian businessman and politician Atiku Abubakar.

Patrol officers in the (DC) Metropolitan Police Department's 6-D division took me on a "ride-along" east of the river. They educated me directly, by answering all my questions, and indirectly, by letting me watch them in action as they performed "armed social work" in support of our city's residents.

I try to honor with my work my late mentors who taught me how to think, write, and fight for my conclusions about what's right: my parents

Clinton and Mary Crane Rossiter, Cornell professors Arch Dotson and Jerry Ziegler, congressional Arms Control and Foreign Policy executive director Edie Wilkie, economist and anti-war teach-in leader Bob Browne, and Center for International Policy directors Don Ranard and Bob White. They also taught me to respect people with whom I disagree and— *pace* Voltaire— to defend to the death their right to speak.

Finally, what would this man be without this woman, Maya Latynski? In 1984 I asked her, "May I hope?" Now I hope that she never wakes up and smells the coffee.